W9-BHB-665

MYSTERY
of the
GREEN CAT

Westminster Press books by
PHYLLIS A. WHITNEY

The Mystery of the Gulls
The Island of Dark Woods
Mystery of the Black Diamonds
Mystery on the Isle of Skye
Mystery of the Green Cat

MYSTERY
of the
GREEN CAT

by

Phyllis A. Whitney

with Illustrations by
Richard Horwitz

Philadelphia
THE WESTMINSTER PRESS

COPYRIGHT, MCMLVII, BY PHYLLIS A. WHITNEY

All rights reserved — no part of this book
may be reproduced in any form without permission in writing from the publisher, except
by a reviewer who wishes to quote brief passages in connection with a review in magazine or newspaper.

Library of Congress Catalog Card Number: 57-5435

PRINTED IN THE UNITED STATES OF AMERICA

CONTENTS

1

TWO BROTHERS AND TWO SISTERS

WITHOUT leaving his place by the wide living room window, Andy could hear angry sounds coming from across the hall. A slamming of drawers and a general banging was going on in the bedroom Andy shared with his twin brother, Adrian.

Andy tried to focus his attention on the view of San Francisco Bay, shining blue-gold this Sunday afternoon in July. Their home until a short time ago had been low on another hillside, with no glimpse of the bay. Andy liked to look over the roof tops of San Francisco and watch cars speeding across the Bay Bridge to Oakland on the opposite shore. He liked to see the boats, big and small, moving about on the water and all the lively bustle of a big city on the streets below.

Adrian, however, had never wanted to leave their old house. That house had been one last tie with their mother. Even the furniture in this place was new. Only Mom's baby grand piano was familiar. Emily, their new stepmother, didn't play. The piano was here for Adrian, who never touched it any more.

Upstairs on the second level Dad and Emily were

moving about, getting ready to go to the airport. Andy hoped they couldn't hear Adrian slamming things around. Maybe he'd better try to calm his brother down a bit.

Andy went to the door and looked in. Adrian's fair hair was rumpled as if he had been combing it straight up with his fingers in irritation, and his gray eyes looked as stormy as the bay did on an overcast day. Once more Andy was struck by the difference between them. Nobody ever thought they were twins. Adrian was taller and thinner and had all the good looks. Andy didn't care about looks — that sort of thing was for girls — but when he grew up he wanted to be tall like his father, and Adrian was getting there first.

" You trying to shake the house down? " Andy asked his brother good-naturedly.

His answer was a metallic crash as Adrian swept his arm across a table, knocking Andy's tools to the floor.

" Can't you keep your monkey wrenches and junk in the garage? " his brother demanded. " If we've got to share a room as small as this, you can at least keep out stuff that ought to be someplace else."

Andy was both dismayed and startled. When Mom was alive, Adrian, in spite of occasional moods, had been pretty even-tempered. A swell brother, really — awfully smart and talented. Andy had always looked up to him secretly. But now everything seemed wrong and Adrian was changing in a frightening sort of way.

Feeling guilty, Andy knelt to pick up his tools. He had meant to take them back to the racks in the garage. In his own room in the other house nobody had complained if he brought half the garage in. Mom had never objected when he had some invention he was tinkering with. But Adrian had a tidy streak — except when it came to his painting stuff. Already there were glasses and brushes spread out on the window ledge. Andy didn't point that out, however. He went toward the door, trying to make his words sound casual as he spoke.

" You won't be ready to leave for the airport, if you don't get out of those jeans pretty soon."

" I'm not going," Adrian said shortly.

Andy stopped in the doorway. " But — Emily expects you — " It was hard to call his stepmother by her first name when he hardly knew her. Though what else was there to call her? He agreed with Adrian that they certainly couldn't call her " Mom " or " Mother." Up until two years ago someone else had that name. The hurt of knowing his mother was gone still ached inside Andy and he didn't mean to put anyone else in her place. Just the same, his father's new wife seemed such an eager-to-be-liked, young sort of person. He didn't want to hurt her feelings. Adrian was already making it hard for her.

" I don't care what she expects." Adrian never used her name if he could get out of it. He pulled on his jacket and reached for his sketching kit. " I'm going out before they come downstairs. What do I care about going to meet *her* daughters? "

Andy didn't want to meet a couple of girls either — there were more interesting things to do. Girls giggled about nothing. They were always looking in mirrors and fussing about their clothes. Adrian could talk to them well enough when he wanted to, but Andy never knew what to say to a girl. Especially, he wouldn't know what to say to *these* girls, and that made him all the more anxious for Adrian to come. It was only because his father and Emily wanted it so much tha Andy was going to the airport.

" Dad won't like it if you don't go," he pointed out.

" I don't care," said Adrian defiantly. " We did't ask for this whole new family to be shoved in on us. If there weren't two girls coming, we could each have our own room, the way we did before."

Adrian brushed past Andy and went out the back door, slamming it on the way. Andy ran after his brother. Adrian couldn't go off like this without a word to Dad.

" Hey — wait a minute! " he called.

Adrian paused on the rear terrace that edged a tiny garden. His thin face had the pinched look anger gave it, and the mouth that could smile so appealingly was twisted as if something hurt him.

" It's no use, Andy. Tell Dad there was something I had to do. You can be the welcome committee if you want, but not me." He breathed hard, and his gaze moved to the big hilltop house on a level higher than theirs. " Maybe Her Highness up there will start throwing things again and give the girls a good scare. I hope she does! So long, Andy."

There was no way to stop his brother. Andy sighed and looked up at the old house above, with its curlicue towers and dormer windows sticking out every which way. It was queer to think of a baroness living up there — if she really was a baroness. He'd never seen her close up — only from a distance. She was awfully old and she never left the house. The other old lady she lived with got around a bit, though she did not speak to anyone she met on the road. They were a funny pair.

The lower windows of the rear tower were empty now. For once no old woman sat there watching. Of course Adrian didn't understand about the baroness throwing things. He didn't know about the queer business of the green cat. For some reason Andy had felt like protecting that silver-haired old lady from his brother's scorn and he had kept the truth of what had happened to himself.

Well, he might as well go back inside, since he hadn't been able to stop his brother. In a way he could sympathize with Adrian's feelings. This whole thing had been pretty surprising. Dad had been as broken up about Mom's death as his sons had been. He'd thrown himself harder than ever into work on the newspaper where he did feature articles. And he'd seemed so lost and lonely that sometimes Andy had found himself trying to comfort his father. Both Andy and Adrian had been shocked when Dad brought this girl home from New York to introduce her to the boys before they were married. Even the letter Dad had written ahead of time hadn't helped to ease the hurt of knowing their mother could be forgotten like this.

Dad explained in the letter that since her husband's death a number of years before, Emily Spencer had been a fashion artist. She drew pictures of chubby little

children for store advertising. He had sent some clip-
pings of her drawings home and Adrian was snooty
about them. Anybody could draw stuff like that, he
pointed out to his brother. This sort of commercial
work didn't make a person an artist. Nevertheless,
Andy, who could not even draw a ball so it looked like
one, had thought the pictures in the ads sort of cute.

Now Dad and Emily were married and back from
their honeymoon. Mrs. Fox, the housekeeper who had
taken care of the twins since Mom's death, had gone to
another job. They'd all moved into this house on Russian Hill, and of course Emily's two daughters were
coming to live here. After all, what else could she do
with them?

Absent-mindedly, Andy picked up a small double
frame that held two enlarged snapshots. The little girl
with the long fluffy hair was Carol. She was only eight
and in this picture she was dressed in a dance costume
representing a butterfly. Emily said Carol loved to
dance and that it would be a good thing to have throw
rugs on the living room floor, so she could put them
aside when she wanted to practice.

Andy shuddered at the thought of this kid fluttering
around underfoot pretending she was a butterfly or
something. He almost wished he could follow Adrian
and run away. The other girl was twelve — just a year
younger than Andy and Adrian. She didn't look as
pretty as her little sister. Her hair was darker and close-
cropped. In this picture she was squinting at the sun
and you couldn't tell much about her. The fact that she
was a girl was bad enough. Why couldn't one of Emily's
kids have been a boy?

He heard his father's step on the stairs and put the pictures down quickly.

Roger Dallas must have looked a bit like Adrian when he was young though he was dark where Adrian was brightly fair as their mother had been. Andy thought Dad pretty distinguished-looking, with his dark hair, gray-streaked at the temples, and his tall, erect figure.

" Where is Adrian? " his father asked, coming down into the living room from the stairs at the rear.

" He — he had something to do," Andy said hesitantly. " He can't make it to the airport."

" So he ran out on us, did he? " Mr. Dallas said. He looked more sad than angry.

Andy could only nod. His stepmother came lightly down the stairs in her high-heeled red shoes, and he couldn't say anything more.

" Well, let's hurry along," his father said. " We don't want to be late for the airport. Sorry, Em, but I guess we'll have to leave without Adrian. He gets sudden notions like this — they don't mean anything."

Emily Spencer Dallas had curly, light-brown hair that framed her pert face in little wisps. Her eyes were big and brown and sometimes, as Andy had noted, they could look worried, even when she was smiling. They looked that way now, and it was because of Adrian. Andy didn't know whether his brother suspected it or not, but Emily seemed a little bit afraid of Adrian. He certainly hadn't done a thing to make her welcome as Dad had asked them both to do.

As Andy closed the garage door for Dad, he glanced up at the house on the hill again and saw that the silver-haired old lady was back in her place on the first floor of the corner tower. She was watching through her binoculars as usual. Adrian said she was an old snoop who ought to be reported to the police. But somehow Andy didn't mind her interest. Maybe she was lonesome up there. He was tempted to wave to her, but he didn't quite dare. That green-cat business had been a little scary.

" Come along, son," his father called, and he hurried to get into the front seat with Emily and his father.

Some distance away a plane was coming in toward San Francisco International Airport in the late afternoon. In one of the rear seats two girls were trying to look out the same window at once. The older one with the short dark hair had a concerned look in her brown eyes. The fluffy-haired eight-year-old was excited and happy.

" Do you think we can see Mommy from the air when we fly in? " Carol asked her sister.

Jill shook her head. " She'll be too small. But she wrote that she'd be waiting for us as close to the gate as she could get."

" I miss her," Carol said simply. " Jill, do you think it will be different now? "

" How do you mean — different? " Jill asked cautiously. She didn't want her own uneasiness to reach her sister.

" Well — I mean we'll have brothers. Do you think Mommy will get to like them better than she does us? "

Jill put an arm around her sister and hugged her almost fiercely. " Of course not. It's like she wrote us —

that we'll just be a bigger family than we were before."

" Maybe it will be fun to have brothers," Carol said philosophically. She was usually ready to take a hopeful, sunny attitude toward whatever happened to her.

Jill was not so sure. All her best friends in New York, and at her grandmother's in Connecticut, had been girls. Some of them had brothers, but mostly the brothers made Jill uncomfortable. When she tried to be nice and wanted to play their games, they made faces and told her to beat it. As often as not they teased her and made fun of her. It wasn't that she didn't want boys to like her — but somehow she always managed to do the wrong thing when there was a boy around.

It was far from reassuring that the Spencer girls were now to live in the same house with twin brothers. Twins meant that whatever was bad about one boy would be repeated in the other. And that sounded like double trouble. True, in the snapshots their father had sent, these twins didn't look much alike. But they were both boys, and that was alarming enough.

The electric sign above the door at the end of the aisle warned passengers to fasten their seat belts. Carol left the window reluctantly and plumped into her seat on the aisle. They'd taken turns at the window all the way across the country and, since Carol had the window for the last take-off, it was Jill's turn now.

Even with her seat belt fastened, Jill could see out the window and down onto the water they were crossing. Her stomach felt jittery. It would be only a little while now until everything must be faced.

Carol tugged suddenly at her sister's sleeve. " Jill,

what do we call him? Nobody said what we should call him."

Jill knew what her sister meant. She had worried about this too. Of course Carol could hardly remember their father because he had died when she was just two. Even Jill could remember him only a little. But because their mother had talked about him such a lot, and they knew all the pictures of him by heart, they had the feeling of knowing him. The smiling man in these pictures was Daddy, and no one else could ever be that to the girls.

"We better just call him ' Mr. Dallas ' to begin with," Jill decided. "After all, we don't know him very well."

"Anyway, I like him," said Carol happily. " He doesn't scare me a bit."

Jill liked him too. The tall, fine-looking man, who had taken them out several times while he was in New York, had seemed understanding and friendly. No, it wasn't Mr. Dallas who worried Jill. It was his two un-known sons who would probably be with him waiting for the passengers from this plane to disembark.

The plane was dropping down now. Jill couldn't see the airport, so they must be flying directly toward it. Before she knew it there was the airstrip racing along below them. In seconds the wheels bumped gently on the concrete and the propellors made a whirring sound as the plane braked and cut its speed. Smoothly they rolled toward the handsome terminal buildings of the San Francisco airport.

And now Jill felt more jittery than ever.

2

OBSERVER ON THE WALL

WISPS of fog were drifting in overhead, but not thick enough yet to obscure the sun. Jill took deep breaths of the bracing air that was so wonderful to drink in after the air-conditioned plane.

" There's Mommy! " Carol cried.

Jill caught sight of a red hat shining in the sunlight and hurried toward her mother right on Carol's heels. She had no time to do more than glance at the tall man and the stocky boy beside him before she and Carol were swept together into their mother's arms. Carol was crying openly with happiness, and there were tears on Jill's cheeks too, though she wasn't sure whether they were her own or her mother's.

Somehow this first look was reassuring. Mother had worn her red shoes and little red hat — the combination she picked for happy occasions. And she didn't look one bit different. Being Mrs. Roger Dallas didn't seem to have changed her in the least. She was Mother to her daughters and that was all that mattered.

Jill could hardly speak for the gulpy feeling in her throat as her mother turned them about to greet Mr.

Dallas and the boy who stood behind his father in an uneasy sort of way. Mr. Dallas had the good sense not to hug them, though probably Carol wouldn't have minded. Jill wanted to go more slowly with this stranger who was now her stepfather. She put her hand gravely into his, and he took it in a comfortably friendly way.

" Welcome home," he said. " This is my son Andrew. Andy, this is Jill and Carol."

Andy grunted something that might be taken for " Hi," but he didn't say anything else. It was plain that this boy had not looked forward to their coming and wasn't going to put himself out to talk to them.

When Mr. Dallas had collected the baggage and loaded it in the back of the car, he opened the door to the rear seat.

" Suppose you get in back with Andy and Carol, Em, and I'll take Jill up in front with me."

A faint prickle of resentment went through Jill. She belonged in back with Mother too. But Mother obeyed at once — almost too readily — and Carol cuddled right into the seat beside her. There was nothing for Jill to do but get in front with Mr. Dallas. At least it was nice to have a car in the family. They hadn't had one in New York City.

The road ran along below a row of tawny hills dotted with little white houses. The traffic on the highway was busy, and Mr. Dallas kept his eye on the road, talking to Jill as he drove.

" I'm glad to have you up here with me so I can give you a bit of an introduction to San Francisco on the way in," he said. " This is a city you'll like when you get to know it."

This sounded friendly and Jill felt better about having to give up her place beside her mother to Andy.

As they drove along, Mr. Dallas indicated various points of interest, but Jill had a feeling that all the while his mind was on something else, something that was worrying him. They crossed Market Street — the long street that ran clear from Twin Peaks to the Ferry Building on the Bay — before Mr. Dallas came to the point.

" I want to tell you a little about the other twin, Adrian," he said quietly. " I'm sorry he couldn't come to the airport with us, but he's busy on some school project right now."

" School? " said Jill in surprise. " But this is summertime."

" He's taking morning art classes five days a week," Mr. Dallas explained. " And he likes to go sketching on Sunday. So he keeps busy all summer. I hope, Jill, that you'll give him a little time to get used to two girls, and not take it seriously if he doesn't seem friendly at first. He makes friends more slowly than Andy."

Since Andy hadn't made friends at all, this was somewhat alarming. " You mean he doesn't want us here? " Jill asked bluntly.

" I wouldn't put it that way," Mr. Dallas said in a low voice so that Andy wouldn't hear. " You see, the boys lost their mother just two years ago. We've been a pretty lonely household ever since. We've needed a woman in our home again, but Adrian doesn't altogether realize that. He was very much attached to his mother and perhaps he will be a little resentful of your mother at first. I want to talk to you about this because you're older than your sister and better able to understand. Adrian's a good kid, really, and very talented, though perhaps too sensitive. I'll be grateful if you'll do your best to make friends with him."

How was she to make friends with someone who didn't want her there in the first place? Jill wondered. But Mr. Dallas sounded kind and a little sad and Jill warmed to him, wanted to please him.

" I — I'll try," she said uncertainly.

His smile told her he liked her. " I know you will. Thanks, Jill. Besides, we can never tell what Adrian will do. Everything may be quite all right."

Jill certainly hoped so. But why was all his father's concern about Adrian? What about the silent boy in the back seat?

Now Mr. Dallas was pointing out the buildings and hills of San Francisco. There were a lot of hills, he explained, but probably three main ones. Nob Hill was up there on their right. Telegraph Hill was beyond, with the big white Coit Tower on its top. They couldn't see it from here. The Dallas house was on Russian Hill — the highest of all.

Mother heard him and sat forward on the edge of the seat to put a hand on Jill's shoulder. There was love in her touch and Jill felt close to her again.

" There's the most wonderful view from our house," she said, sliding back again. " We're perched right near the top of the hill. There's only one house higher up.

That's a mystery house and I know how you love mysteries. Jill's our bookworm, Roger."

"Good," said Mr. Dallas. "I like both books and bookworms. There are plenty of good stories about San Francisco among our books at home, Jill."

"What's mysterious about the house?" Jill asked, her interest caught. It was true that she loved any sort of mystery — either in a story or in real life. The trouble was that no one ever met a real mystery in everyday life.

Andy spoke for the first time. "There's a baroness living up there."

"That's only neighborhood gossip," his father said. "The other old lady, Miss Furness, seems to refer to her simply as Mrs. Wallenstein."

"But what's the mystery?" Jill persisted.

Mr. Dallas smiled sympathetically at her eagerness. "Practically everything about that house and the two women who live there is a mystery to me. I didn't know we were moving next door to a couple of San Francisco recluses. I believe that old house goes back to before the earthquake and fire in 1906. But the two old ladies keep so much to themselves that not even the neighbors know much about them. I have a feeling their story might be a good one to write up sometime. That is, if they didn't mind."

Now the car was climbing the steep rise of Russian Hill and Mother said eagerly: "Ours is the next turn. We live on a little blind street with only a few houses on it."

Jill forgot about the mystery, interested in more immediate reality. The approach to the house was over the rise of a hill and down a steep short street. The street ended in a cement wall and the hill dropped sharply away below. Everywhere houses crowded the hillside, but there was room for plenty of greenery too. Fluffy tree foliage framed some of the roof tops, and flowers grew everywhere.

There was a brief glimpse of hills and roof tops and water beyond, before Mr. Dallas swung the wheel of the car and turned sharply into a drive that ran past a low house built against the steep hillside.

Andy got out of the car to open the garage door and the girls and their mother went in the back way, through a bright kitchen, then into a big room that served as both living room and dining room.

Carol squealed with pleasure at the sight of it. " Look how big, Jill! And only little rugs I can kick back. It will be wonderful for dancing."

" Take it easy," Jill said. " Don't start moving the furniture the first minute you're in the house."

Sometimes Jill felt a little impatient over Carol's concentration on dancing. It seemed as though life was always being interrupted to get Carol to or from a dancing lesson, or make her ballet costumes, or just sit and play audience. Jill was proud of her, of course, but sometimes she got tired of hearing people say: " Isn't Carol darling! And so graceful. Like a little fairy." Then they'd look at Jill, who was always falling over her feet and dropping things and getting into trouble. And they wouldn't say anything. Jill dismissed the thought of Carol's dancing with a private snort and followed her mother into the bedroom she and her sister were to share.

There was not much view from the side window of the bedroom. The hill went straight up close to the window and Jill could see the lower part of a high wall belonging to the property above. But out the back window there was a glimpse of the Dallas terrace and postage-stamp garden.

" The door over there is the bathroom, which you'll share with the boys," Mother said. " Their bedroom is just beyond."

Jill looked about the room with appreciation. The twin beds were maple, with gay spreads of green, touched with an occasional rosebud. There was a huge maple dresser with a double row of drawers, which would make dividing easy, and there were even twin maple desks for writing and studying.

" It's lots nicer than the apartment in New York," Carol said and Jill agreed that it was wonderful.

Satisfied that they liked the room, Mother opened her arms and in a minute she was hugging both girls to her and kissing first one, then the other. After that she held them off at arms' length and looked at them hungrily.

" I could eat you both up," she said. " I've missed you so, darlings! You look fine — healthy and brown. And I'll bet you're hungry by now."

Mother's cheeks were pink and her eyes bright. Jill regarded her with love and admiration.

Both girls admitted to the hunger and Mother turned toward the door. " You two get unpacked and I'll start dinner. Baked beans tonight. Does that sound good? "

" Mmm! " said Jill and added, " How is the cooking? "

Mrs. Dallas paused in the doorway, mischief in her eyes. " Ssh! I'm still getting by with a can opener. But don't tell."

" No experiments? " Jill asked, laughing. In New York, Mother had so little time to cook after work that mostly she used frozen things and mixes and cans. Canned baked beans, fixed up with onions and catchup and Worcestershire sauce, could be yummy good. But Mother had never been much interested in cooking unless some really adventurous recipe tempted her. These she termed " experiments," and the fact that they seldom came out successfully never kept her from trying the next fancy dish.

Mother shook her head, sobering. " No experiments. I haven't dared. It seems that the boys' mother was a wonderful cook and I get nervous every time I step into the kitchen. But, with you two here to give me moral support, maybe I'll get up my courage to try something ambitious. Like an apple pie. Adrian says his mother made awfully good apple pie. And no mixes."

She went off and in a few minutes Mr. Dallas and Andy brought in the bags. The girls began to unpack and hang up their clothes. The closet was big and they divided sides and overhead shelves, just as they had done in the apartment back home. But there was more room now. Carol hummed happily and did a *pas-de-bourrée* from suitcase to closet, and a couple of *jetés* back to the bed where her suitcase was balanced.

Jill was less interested in unpacking and impatient to
finish so she could look around the house and get ac-
quainted with their new surroundings.

" You're stuffing! " said Carol critically as Jill bent
over a bureau drawer. " Everything will be wrinkled if
you do that."

Jill paid no attention. It was speed that counted right
now. She paused by the rear window while she fitted a
dress crookedly on a hanger and looked up at the hill
above. There seemed to be two levels of walls up there.
The lower level slanted toward the street, as if it hid
a passageway. The upper wall was high and concealed
the garden from this angle, except for the tops of a few
trees. Both walls looked crumbly and old, with bits of
moss growing between the stones and all sorts of shrubbery and vines, like uncombed locks of hair, hanging
over the top. The house itself was a dingy weather-
beaten brown in color, and gloomily weird in appearance. Towers and cupolas and high balconies defied
order, though Jill thought they looked terribly interesting.

As Jill stared at the closed shutters and blank windows of the house, a slight movement near the upper
wall attracted her attention. She saw hands part the
green stuff that overhung the wall. Slowly the top of a
head came into view, and eyes peered through the
shrubbery. This could not be the old lady Andy and
his father had mentioned. The bobbed hair was very
black and straight and there were straight black bangs
across the forehead. Beneath the bangs were a pair of

winged black eyebrows and lively dark eyes. That was all Jill could see. The observer from the wall climbed no higher, but seemed to be searching the Dallas garden before finally looking toward the house. Jill remained in plain view at the window and suddenly the watcher saw her. There was an instant in which the two stared at each other. Then the head vanished, the shrubbery sprang back into place, and nothing else moved in the grounds above.

Jill looked in surprise at the place where the head had emerged. How very queer! Who could be so secretly interested in what went on down here? Feeling completely mystified, Jill was about to leave the window to tell Carol what she had seen, when another movement caught her eye.

This time it was someone in the Dallas garden. A boy had come around the side of the house. He was tall and slim and had a golden, shining look about him. As he turned slowly toward the house Jill caught her breath. He was the best-looking boy she had ever seen in her life. Why — he looked like the painting of Sir Galahad she remembered from a picture book long ago. Sir Galahad in blue jeans.

" What are you staring at? " Carol asked, coming to stand beside her. She spied the boy too and watched with her sister.

He looked up and saw them. For a moment he returned their stare coolly, without greeting or recognition.

" That must be Adrian! " Carol cried and waved to him unhesitatingly.

The boy did not return her gesture. He looked in-differently away and as he came toward the back door of the house, Jill saw that his blond brows were drawn down in a faint scowl.

" What's the matter with him? " Carol asked.

" I don't know," said Jill. She returned to her un-packing, moving more slowly and thoughtfully now.

This was the boy whom Mr. Dallas had asked her to make friends with. It was startling how different he was from his twin, Andy. He looked interesting — more interesting than Andy, in spite of his rude behavior. But, if he was ready to dislike her before she even spoke to him, what could she do?

3

THE BROKEN WINDOW

WHEN Jill had more or less finished the clothes-jumbling she termed unpacking, she went out to the kitchen to see if she could help her mother. The oven was on and she could smell the baked beans heating up. Mother had changed her red shoes for braided green and yellow sandals and she wore a bright yellow apron over her beige dress. She was pretty, Jill thought, with love welling up in her heart, and looked younger than anybody else's mother. For a second Jill was curious about what the twins' mother had been like. Surely she couldn't have been as special as her mother.

The kitchen was done in pale, shining gray, with bright touches of red in window curtains, working surfaces, and linoleum. Red geraniums were on the window sill above the sink.

Mrs. Dallas bent to open the oven door to peek in, checking things off as she did so. " Baked beans are easy. Meat loaf — that's easy too. I'm a great success with meat loaf. Baked potatoes — elementary. Pineapple and cottage cheese salad, with nuts on top — a natural. Ice cream for dessert. This will be the third time this week that we've had ice cream. I hope I'm not overdoing it."

" With grated chocolate on top? " Carol asked, popping into the kitchen just then. She had changed from the wrinkled dress she had worn on the plane to a red and black cotton plaid and looked pretty and neat. Jill had forgotten to change.

Mother gestured with her head, both hands busy. " A good idea. You can grate the chocolate, Carol. You'll find the grater on the ledge over there. And, Jill, you can begin to learn where things are by helping me set the table."

Jill was glad to be given a task. Through the open door into the living room she could see Mr. Dallas on the couch, reading the paper, while Andy lay stretched full length on the floor studying the funnies. Jill had felt shy about going into the room without something to keep her busy. Adrian was nowhere in sight when she carried in some plates, and she was both disappointed and relieved. Roger Dallas looked up as she came in and his smile made her welcome.

This time she took a longer look at the living room and liked what she saw. It was big and went off into a little ell at one end. Her mother's taste for modern furnishings showed in the attractive and comfortable chairs and couch, low tables and stream-lined lamps. There was lots of chocolate brown, with gay touches of yellow and green for contrast. On the mantel above the fireplace were several familiar ornaments from home in New York. Only the big old piano seemed out of place. Jill wondered if the boys played.

Once as she went back and forth between the long modern dining table and the kitchen, carrying Mother's dark green plastic dishes, she had to set things down and go across to the big window that looked out over San Francisco. As Mother had said, the view was wonderful. Fog floated thinly overhead, but you could see through it to blue sky and billows of summer clouds high above. The evening was still light, but here and there lights were on in the houses that crowded all about, up and down the hills.

Andy left his funny papers and came to stand beside her. " That's the Coit Tower over on Telegraph Hill," he said almost shyly. " You can go right to the top of it and see all over San Francisco."

Jill nodded, equally shy, but glad that he had spoken to her. When she went back to her table-setting she thought about how hard it was to talk to somebody new, especially a boy. Did boys, she wondered, feel that way about talking to a new girl too?

Mother came in with a small black bowl in her hands, filled with red geraniums from the garden.

" Have you ever seen anything like California geraniums? " she asked, holding up the bowl. " They're giants. And I love the spicy smell."

Jill sniffed, agreeing. The black bowl and red flowers looked beautiful in the middle of the table.

" I thought geraniums were for outdoors," said a new voice behind her and Jill turned to see that Adrian had come into the room from the hall. He had changed from jeans to gray slacks and close up he seemed taller than ever. His face looked thinner and rather pinched in.

His father glanced up from his paper. " No reason for not bringing them into the house that I can think of," he said cheerfully. " Adrian, this is Jill Spencer. Carol is out in the kitchen. Since you couldn't accompany us to the airport, you might step out there and meet her."

Jill said, " Hello," feeling a little flustered, and Adrian said, " How do you do," stiffly polite.

Carol had heard her name and came in quickly, moving with her light, dancing step. The smile she gave Adrian would have disarmed an ogre and he couldn't altogether resist her.

" Gee, but you're tall! " Carol said and looked pertly up at him.

Adrian smiled faintly as he sat down on the couch beside his father, but the smile did not include Jill.

Mother came to the door, swishing off her apron. Her cheeks were still pink and she looked a little excited as she did sometimes when she had company and came to what she called " the crisis point " of serving dinner.

" Everything's ready," she said. And then quickly to Jill as they came to the table: " No — not there beside Carol. Let's mix things up a bit. Roger and I will take the end places, but you sit beside Adrian on this side, Jill. And Carol and Andy can sit opposite."

Andy thumped into his chair at once, primarily interested in food, but Adrian pulled his stepmother's chair out with a stiff gesture and seated her. Then he came silently to take his place next to Jill, who might as well have been invisible as far as he was concerned. Goodness, but he was mad about something.

Mother did her best at conversation, and Mr. Dallas told a lively story about his work at the office, but it was nevertheless an awkward meal. Only Carol seemed unconscious of any undercurrents and chattered un-self-consciously until Jill wished she'd be quiet. Andy ate with enthusiasm and asked for more, but that was his only comment. Adrian stared at his plate and only picked at his food. Jill, watching the two boys warily, felt her own appetite fading. She could see how bright her mother's eyes were, and how anxious she looked. Mother was trying too hard to be nice to the boys, and Jill wished she could think of something to say to break up an awkward silence.

"A funny thing happened a little while ago," she began desperately.

Andy and Adrian both stared at her as if one of the cups had started to talk. But Mr. Dallas came to her aid before she could choke back her words.

"What was that?" he asked with interest. "Anything to do with our neighbors on the hill?"

"I suppose it was one of the neighbors," Jill said. "Somebody climbed halfway up the highest wall and peeked down at us through the bushes."

Andy grinned. "That wasn't the baroness. I think she must be an invalid because she stays inside all the time. And Miss Furness, the other old lady, doesn't go around climbing walls."

"This person had bobbed black hair and black

bangs," Jill went on. " And she was certainly interested in what was going on down here."

" They're all snoops up there," Adrian said shortly.

" It must have been the Japanese girl," Andy said. " A Japanese family that works for the baroness lives in part of the house. The man seems to take care of the gardening and house chores, and I guess the woman cooks and cleans."

" Looks like our neighbors aren't the only snoopy ones," his father said, teasing. " You seem to know all about the affairs up there."

Andy flushed, but he went on doggedly. " I don't think being interested is being snoopy. Anyway, I've seen the girl around a few times since we moved in. Once I tried to speak to her, but she acted bashful and had a funny way of talking."

" There's another mystery for you to solve, Jill," Mother said, eager to keep the conversation going.

Jill wished Mother hadn't brought up that mystery business before Adrian. He looked as if he might think such things childish. It was Carol who saved the day by changing the subject in her own frank manner.

" Mr. Dallas," she said, " what are we supposed to call you? Jill and I talked about it on the plane, and we don't really know."

Jill wriggled in her chair and bit her lip. This was being uncomfortably outspoken. But Mr. Dallas seemed to accept Carol's question without surprise.

" That's something your mother and I have wondered about," he said. " We'd like you to call us whatever seems to fit best. Perhaps ' Emily ' seems easier to say than ' Roger ' — especially since Emily is a bit closer to your age than I am. But I feel that ' Mister ' sounds a little stiff. Have any of you a notion on the subject? "

" Maybe we could use nicknames," Andy suggested.

However, since neither of the grownups seemed to have nicknames, this idea languished and a silence fell again upon the table. Jill tried repeating " Roger " in her own mind, but it didn't sound right and she was afraid she could never bring herself to use it.

She was glad of a chance to help her mother carry out dishes before dessert. Andy would have helped too, but Mother waved him back to his seat.

" This is a job you can take turns at, if you like," she suggested. " Jill can help clear the table tonight. Then I'd like a volunteer dish wiper, if anyone wants to help me on that."

Adrian said nothing, but Andy bragged that he was awfully good at dish wiping and never broke more than four or five plates a meal. That at least set them laughing.

It was while they were eating ice cream, with Carol's grated chocolate over the top, that Jill noticed a water color painting that hung over the mantel. It showed a busy scene of docks and fishing boats, with a little boy in the foreground holding up a crab. On a shed behind him a row of sea gulls watched.

" That looks interesting," Jill said. " Is it a scene around San Francisco? "

" A very well known scene," Mr. Dallas agreed. " Fisherman's Wharf. We'll have to take you and Carol down there one of these days. Adrian painted that picture."

"My mother had it framed," Adrian added stonily.

Jill stared at him in admiration. "You must be a very good artist."

"I don't like that painting," he said, and concentrated on sprinkling more chocolate on his ice cream.

His father only laughed. "Adrian is a perfectionist, Jill. He thinks anything he painted yesterday is terrible and wants to throw it away. It's all I can do to get him to show me his work because he's so critical of it."

Mother came quickly to Adrian's defense. "That seems a good way to be. When we're satisfied with what we do, our critical faculties have usually gone to sleep."

Adrian said nothing, and Carol chose that moment to make another frank statement.

"My mother is an artist," she told the boys proudly. "She draws better than almost anybody."

Mother said: "Hush, dear. I'm afraid you're prejudiced. I'm not in Adrian's class at all."

What might have been said next, they were never to know, because at that moment a crash of breaking glass sounded from the rear of the house.

For an instant they stared at one another in shocked surprise. Then they all pushed away from the table in a flurry and rushed into the little hall. The sound had come from the girls' bedroom and Jill and Andy got there first.

A pane in the side window which looked out on the steep hill above had been shattered. Broken glass lay scattered upon the carpet and slivers of it had fallen

on Jill's bed. It was Andy who picked up the rock that
lay on the floor not far from the broken window. He
held it out on his palm for them to see.

"So she's throwing stones again," said Adrian so
quietly that only Jill and Andy heard him.

Mother looked a little frightened, while Mr. Dallas
was plainly angry.

"That rock could only have come from the hill
above," he said. "And there's nothing up there except

that old house. Well — our baroness is going to have a phone call from me right now! "

He went off to the living room telephone. Mother, Adrian, and Carol hurried after him, but Andy stood where he was, staring at the big rock he held in his hand. Jill remained behind to question him.

" Do you think somebody really tossed it through our window to be mean? " she asked. " Is there some one up there who wants to hurt us? "

Andy didn't answer directly. There was a puzzled look on his plain, tanned face as he stared at the rock.

" Have you ever heard of a green cat? " he asked Jill.

4

VISITOR FROM THE UPHILL HOUSE

JILL was as startled by Andy's question as she had been by the broken window.

" A green cat? Of course not. What do you mean? "

Andy didn't answer. He went to the window and stared up at the walls and hillside above. Then he shook his head.

" The other one landed on the back terrace," he said.

" You mean people up there have thrown rocks at you before? "

Andy nodded, but he looked uneasy. " Don't say anything. I didn't tell Dad about the other time. Only Adrian knows, and he hasn't mentioned it. I asked him not to."

" But why shouldn't he mention it? If someone up there is dangerous, I should think you'd report it to the police."

" Listen! " Andy said.

He went into the hall and Jill followed him. They could hear Mr. Dallas speaking on the telephone.

" I wish to speak to Mrs. — er — Wallenstein," he said.

There was a silence while the person on the other end of the wire answered. Andy and Jill tiptoed into the living room to hear. Mother sat on the sofa, her knees clasped in her hands, while Carol, her eyes big and round, leaned against her mother's arm. Even Adrian was interested this time. When Andy came to the door Adrian stared at him questioningly. Andy merely shook his head. There was certainly something peculiar afoot here, Jill thought.

Mr. Dallas was speaking again. " Very well, Miss Furness. I'll be glad to explain. Someone from your grounds has thrown a large rock through a bedroom window down here and — "

Though she couldn't distinguish the words, Jill could hear a sputter of indignation at the other end of the wire.

" Now just a moment, Miss Furness," Mr. Dallas broke in. " There's no use becoming excited. All I ask is that you look into the matter. I'm not accusing anyone. But if there are prowlers in your grounds throwing stones down the hill, you ought to know about it."

Again the line sputtered. Then there was a loud click and sudden silence. Plainly Miss Furness had hung up. Mr. Dallas stared at the dead receiver for a moment before he put it back on the cradle. He looked both annoyed and amused.

" I'm afraid that one is rather a tartar," he told Mother. " She said Mrs. Wallenstein couldn't come to the phone, that I was speaking to Matilda Furness and she is head of the household."

"What did she say about the stone?" Mother asked.

Mr. Dallas made a wry face. "Only that I'd taken leave of my senses and such a thing couldn't possibly have happened. I was going to invite her down to have a look, but she hung up before I got a chance. I don't like to refer the matter to the police at this point."

"I agree," Mother said. "We don't want trouble with the neighbors. Perhaps it was an accident."

Mr. Dallas was doubtful. "An accident when it came with a force like that?"

"I think the baroness, whoever she is, is off her rocker," Adrian said. "They probably keep her locked up just so she won't do things like this."

"Now, now," Mr. Dallas said, "let's not jump to conclusions. It's true, Emily, that we don't want to squabble with the neighbors. And perhaps Miss Furness, now that she has been warned, will take care of the matter, whether she admits to us that it happened or not. So I'm willing to let this go unless it occurs again."

"We'll move Jill's bed away from the window," Mother said. "Then we can clean up all that glass."

Mr. Dallas and Adrian went to move the bed. Andy stayed in the living room, still more interested in the rock than in anything else. Jill was curious about what Andy knew.

Suddenly he held out the rock to her. "What does it look like to you?"

Jill took the irregular chunk and turned it about in her fingers. It was about the size of a man's fist. In one place a bit of fuzzy green moss clung to the surface.

" It looks like a broken piece from one of those old walls," Jill said, handing it back to him.

" That's what I think," said Andy. " But somehow I don't believe this has anything to do with the green cat."

Curiosity and bafflement were too much for Jill. " For goodness' sakes — what do you mean about a green cat? "

Andy shook his head in the most maddening way. " I don't know," he said. " I can't figure it out." And that was absolutely all he would say.

The broken window let in quite a lot of air that night. As Jill was discovering, the soft coolness of a summer night in San Francisco was very different from New York's sticky hot humidity. But she slept well and safely in a bed pulled over to a corner away from the window.

Both girls stayed in bed late the next morning, and Mother didn't rouse them. It was nine thirty when Carol, doing *tours jetés* across the bedroom to wake herself up, woke Jill as well. There was no use protesting, Jill knew, as she sat up in bed and rubbed her eyes sleepily. Telling Carol not to dance was like telling a butterfly not to flutter.

In fact, the minute the two had finished breakfast at the bright red-and-chrome table in the kitchen, Carol got out her record player and some ballet records. She tied her fluffy blond hair back in a pony tail, put on ballet slippers, and pushed aside the small rugs on the living room floor.

All the men were out of the house. Mr. Dallas had

gone downtown to his newspaper office, Adrian was at
his art class, and Andy had wandered off with another
boy to look at old pieces of a junked car.

" I understand he invents things," Mother explained
as she and Jill did breakfast dishes. " In fact, he has already fixed me a thingamagig to keep my ironing cord
out of the way. How do you like your new brothers,
Jill? "

Calling them brothers was moving too fast, Jill
thought. So far they were simply two boys whom she
didn't know very well.

"They don't seem very friendly," she admitted.
" Though Andy isn't as standoffish as Adrian."

" I know what you mean," Mother said. " Adrian
is certainly a handsome boy and he has lovely manners,
when he chooses. But it may take him a while to get
used to us, and we'll have to give him time. He really
is talented. Roger showed me some of the paintings
Adrian has discarded and I think he is surprisingly
good. But I haven't found out how to make friends
with him yet. I feel more comfortable with Andy."

Just then the door chimes rang and Jill went to
answer. Carol did not miss a step as she whirled about
the living room. When Jill opened the door she found
a surprising figure on the walk. The girl was tiny and
she wore rolled-up blue jeans, obviously too long for
her, and a shirt of gay green plaid. By her straight
black hair and bangs, Jill knew her for the Japanese
girl who had peeked over the wall the day before. But
now her dark eyes were not dancing with interest and
she wore a most mournful expression.

"Good morning," she said politely. "I am Hana Tamura from house uphill."

Behind Jill, Carol was still dancing and the Japanese girl's eyes followed her in fascination. Jill looked about for help, but, since Mother was nowhere in sight, she invited the visitor in.

Still entranced with Carol, Hana Tamura stepped past Jill into the living room and, at a further invitation, seated herself gingerly on the edge of a chair. Carol, noting that she had an interested audience, threw herself wholeheartedly into her ballet steps. The other two sat in silence watching her.

Mother came into the room just as the music ended and Carol ran to turn the switch on the record player. At once Hana stood up and faced Mother with a quick little bob of her head, repeating the same words she had spoken to Jill. She was such a tiny thing that it was hard to tell how old she was. Not once had she smiled and now she stood gravely before Mother, refusing an invitation to sit down again.

"Prease," she said, changing the "l" to "r", "las' night I do mos' bad thing. I have break window."

In spite of her surprise, Mother smiled. "If you're our culprit, then I'm sure it wasn't intended. Do sit down, Hana, and tell us about it."

Thus urged, Hana sat beside Jill on the couch and began her story hesitantly.

"I am climbing on top wall," she said. "This is not good, but I am mos' wanting to know about new chirren in this house."

"Chirren," Jill gathered, meant "children."

Plainly Hana was not an American-born Japanese.

" I can understand that you'd be interested," Mother said sympathetically.

Hana took a deep breath and went on, her black winged brows drawn down earnestly. " Wall is not so strong. With my foot I have kick loose a stone. It is big stone and it flies off like bird. It strikes on lower wall and goes smash through window. This is bery bad thing and I am hiding myself because Miss Furness will be mos' angry with me."

" But you told her what you had done? " Mother asked gently.

Hana stared at the floor. " No, I do not tell. I am bery ashamed. This morning I tell my father and he is sorry I am so bad. So I come to pay for window. With own money."

Hana dug into the pocket of her jeans, brought up a collection of small coins and held them out to Mother.

" Don't let her pay for it! " Carol pleaded.

Again Mother smiled at Hana. " Of course we won't let you pay, though it is very fine of you to want to. We're glad to know how it happened and that no one was throwing stones at us. But since it was an accident, it's a small matter. Put your money away, Hana."

Hana paid no attention. She placed the small handful of coins proudly on the coffee table.

" Prease," she made an effort and corrected herself, " please, if not enough, I bring more next week. I am making the window broke and I am paying."

Mother knew when she was defeated and Jill was

glad, after all, to see her accept the money. There was a pride about this little Japanese girl that you had to respect.

" Thank you very much, Hana," Mother said. " I'm glad we have such good neighbors."

For the first time the frown of worry lifted from Hana's brows and she smiled shyly, showing straight white teeth. She made a deep, polite bow in Mother's direction and would have gone to the door, but Mrs. Dallas stopped her.

" Wait — don't hurry away, Hana. Why not stay a while and visit with the girls."

The smile left Hana's face and she shook her head. " Thank you bery much, but Miss Furness does not like if I visit neighbors."

" Why not? " Jill asked, disappointed. Hana must be near her own age in spite of her diminutive size. It would be fun to have a new friend — especially since she had never known a Japanese girl before.

Hana looked plainly uneasy. " Miss Furness is saying that neighbors make much trouble and we do not be friends with them."

Again Mother was surprised, but made no further attempt to keep Hana there. Jill saw her to the door and, just as Hana was going down the steps, a thought popped into Jill's mind. Hana might know the answer to a puzzle Andy had brought up.

" Tell me," she said hastily, " do you know anything about a green cat? "

The effect on Hana Tamura was electric. She stared wide-eyed at Jill for a moment. Then she cast a worried

glance toward the big house on the hill above and
scuttled up the road as fast as she could go. Jill watched
her dart through a gate at the end of the passage that
ran behind the lower wall.

So Hana knew something about the green cat, and
whatever it was, it disturbed her!

More curious than ever now, Jill walked up the
road to have a look at the opening through which Hana
had disappeared. A high barred gate closed off the
entrance from the street. Jill could peer between the
bars and see that a narrow passageway led upward
at a slant between the two walls. It curved gently, following the contour of the hill, and went out of sight
at the far end. Passage and gate were rather like the
entrance to a castle.

Just for fun Jill put a hand on the bars of the gate
and pulled, but Hana had bolted it securely after her.
No one could make an entrance to the house of the
baroness here. Not unless an accomplice inside left
the gate unlocked. Jill smiled at her own imaginings.
She was beginning to think like a mystery story — of
secret passages and accomplices. But there was a mystery about that house on the hill and she was growing
more curious about it all the time.

5

JILL MAKES A MISSTEP

WHEN she returned to the house, Mother was remarking to Carol that it was a shame old Miss Furness had to have such odd notions that she wouldn't let her gardener's daughter play with neighborhood children.

" That's really carrying things too far," Mother said. " Perhaps we can persuade her to relax that ruling one of these days."

" Maybe you could ask Miss Furness to let Hana visit us sometime," Jill said. " I really think she wanted to come."

" If I see her perhaps I will," said Mother. " Or if you girls see her first, you can ask her politely yourselves."

Jill doubted that she would have the courage to do that. She hadn't seen the formidable Miss Furness yet, but she was beginning to get the picture of a woman who was rather a dragon.

" If she's only the baroness's housekeeper, I don't see why she's so bossy," Carol said. " I like Hana."

" We don't know that she's a housekeeper," Mother

pointed out. " From what I gather the term ' baroness '
seems to be a nickname for Mrs. Wallenstein. But
Roger says the neighbors around here are mostly new-
comers and they don't know much about the house on
the hilltop. Miss Furness and Mrs. Wallenstein seem
to have been here practically forever and they keep
away from everyone else."

Jill wandered out to the terrace behind the Dallas
house and stared up at the towers and chimneys above.
From here she could see the first floor of the house and
was startled when something light moved at the lower
window of a corner tower. She looked more closely and
saw that a woman with silvery hair sat at the window. It
took Jill a few seconds to realize that the woman was
training a pair of black binoculars directly upon her.
With those glasses, everything on this terrace must seem
practically in the woman's own garden.

Impulse prompted Jill and she waved her hand at
the watcher in the window. For a surprised instant the
glasses were lowered. Then the woman raised her own
hand and waved right back. A moment later she disappeared from the window. If that were Mrs. Wallenstein, she at least was not unfriendly. Jill went into the
house feeling glad that she'd waved.

At noontime Adrian came home for lunch. Andy
had packed some sandwiches to take with him on his
expedition, and Mr. Dallas ate at the office, so there
was just Mother, Carol, Adrian, and Jill at the table.

It seemed a more cheerful meal than dinner had the
night before. Perhaps, Jill thought hopefully, Adrian
was already getting used to them. While they ate,

Mother told him about Hana's visit and how she had brought her own allowance to pay for the broken window. For once Adrian seemed interested.

" She's a funny kid," he said. " I met her one time on the road and I asked her how old she was. She said she was fifteen in Japan, but only fourteen here, which sounds as though she's going backwards."

" I believe the Japanese count themselves one year old at birth," Mother said. " And they have a convenient system of counting everyone one year older on New Year's Day — though I don't expect you'd enjoy doing away with different birthdays. How did your art class go this morning, Adrian? "

Adrian answered readily enough. His work had apparently gone well and he was in a cheerful mood. He was, he told them, very much interested in Oriental art and wanted to make a real study of it. Their brushwork couldn't be surpassed, and he liked the simplicity of line with which Japanese and Chinese artists got their effects.

He sounded as though he might be quoting a book or a teacher, but his audience listened respectfully, only too happy not to have Adrian snubbing them.

"Dad has a good friend downtown at Gump's," he explained. "It's through Mr. Gibbs that I've become interested in the work of Oriental artists."

Carol giggled. "Gump's? What a funny name!"

Adrian was not amused. He explained somewhat reproachfully, that Gump's was a fine old San Francisco store that specialized in valuable jewelry and art objects. They even had a museum of Oriental work upstairs and Adrian had visited it many times. After lunch he might set up a still life to paint in the Oriental manner.

Mother and the two girls were plainly impressed and Adrian seemed to enjoy their interest and attention. If only he would stay like this, Jill thought. Her respect for him was increasing. He sounded so grown up and intelligent when he talked about his work. When lunch was over, Jill tagged around after him somewhat shyly, eager to develop this sign of friendship further.

Unfortunately, Adrian's good mood didn't last. It was the sight of his own room that sent him once more into deep gloom.

"Look at that!" he said angrily.

Jill, standing at his elbow, could see what he meant. Andy was not a tidy roommate and his section of the small room looked as if a magpie had gone through it, strewing articles of various sorts all over the place. It was clear that Andy liked to collect old bottles, bits of scrap iron, corks, and broken pencils. At least those were some of the objects Jill was able to identify. Not everything had been left on Andy's side of the room either. A pair of greasy dungarees had been dropped over the end of Adrian's bed and Adrian picked them up and threw them toward his brother's side of the room.

Certainly this wouldn't be a pleasant room to live in, if Adrian liked things tidy. On the other hand, Jill had a sneaking twinge of sympathy for Andy because she herself was not always a tidy roommate. Especially when she got interested in some new hobby and hated to put things away. Carol was the neat one in their room.

" We had our own rooms before we moved here," Adrian said dismally. " I had a place to work then. But how can I work here? I don't even feel like painting when I look at this mess."

This, thought Jill, accounted for part of the trouble, was part of the cause for Adrian's resentment. And she certainly couldn't blame him.

"Isn't there some place that you could fix up as a sort of — of studio? " she asked hesitantly.

" Where? Just show me where! "

Where indeed, when they seemed to be occupying every inch of the house? Jill went back to the living room and glanced up at the half level of the second story. A decorative, but narrow, balcony hallway overhung the living room, opening into a bedroom which Mr. and Mrs. Dallas shared. Except for a small bathroom up there, no other space was available. The hall downstairs was too small and too dark for studio space. The kitchen was comfortable in size, but Mother needed every inch of it. That left nothing but the living room, which had to serve as dining room too. Though it really was an awfully big living room . . .

Suddenly Jill's imagination was off at full tilt. Since the long living room table was the modern fold-up sort and wasn't left open all the time, that ell was empty except for chairs most of the day. Maybe the table could be set up out in the living room proper when they needed it — which would leave the ell empty. She flew out to the kitchen to consult her mother.

" Adrian needs a place to paint," she announced, and explained her notion.

Mother listened a bit doubtfully at first. But after a moment she nodded. " I don't see why it couldn't be managed. We could try it anyway and see how it works. There'd be a good light for him from the window. And I think I saw a couple of screens put away in the basement storeroom that could be set up to section off that part of the room and make it private."

Jill couldn't wait to tell Adrian. He seemed a little skeptical at first, and not as excited about the idea as she was ready to be. Nevertheless, Mother, Carol, Jill, and Adrian all got busy, moving things around, carrying up screens, helping Adrian bring out his easel and the small table he used for his paints. It was a good thing, he said, that the floor was bare, because sometimes there were spills and he didn't want to be careful all the time. Maybe a linoleum square would be a good idea.

As they carried and arranged, Jill forgot some of the shyness she had felt with him and began to chatter. When Mother and Carol were out of the room, she even told him about Mrs. Wallenstein sitting in the tower window up there, staring through her binoculars.

"I know," Adrian said. "She does that all the time. I think it's pretty nervy. Or else nutty."

"I waved at her," Jill confessed, "and she waved at me. So I don't think she can be so unfriendly."

Adrian stared at Jill. "I wouldn't get chummy with her, if I were you. She threw a rock at Andy and me out on the terrace, you know. It wasn't the Japanese girl that time. I saw her throw it through an open window. Not a big rock — only a pebble. I suppose it wouldn't have hurt if it had hit us. Andy snatched it up and wouldn't show it to me. He's got a soft spot for the loony old thing. But me — I say you'd better stay away from her."

"What did the rock have to do with a green cat?" Jill asked directly.

As before, she got nowhere by mentioning the cat. Adrian looked at her blankly. "What do you mean — green cat?"

So Andy had not confided the private mystery to his brother.

"Oh, nothing," said Jill and turned away too quickly. Her foot struck a vase of brushes she had set on the floor near Adrian's "studio" and sent it flying. There was no water in the jar, but the brushes flew all over the place, the vase struck the metal leg of a chair and broke into bits.

Jill stared at the wreckage in consternation. It seemed as though she had a talent for being clumsy at the worst possible moments. Well, it was a good thing she had broken nothing valuable this time. She had noticed that the vase was already chipped when she carried it in from Adrian's desk in the bedroom. She turned quickly to tell him she was sorry. Maybe Mother would have a jar in the kitchen that would do for his brushes. She tried to suggest this to Adrian, but he wasn't listening.

A flush had come over his thin face, and he looked tragic as he regarded the broken bits of pink and white vase. A little frightened, Jill knelt to pick up the bits, mumbling again that she was sorry. But Adrian kicked the pieces out of her reach furiously.

"Leave them alone!" he cried. "You've done enough damage. My mother gave me that vase for brushes when I went to my first art class. And now it's gone. Like everything else of hers is gone in this house!" He made a gesture around the bright, attractive living room. "There's only the piano left. And I suppose *she* will get rid of that too."

There was such venom in the way he said *she* that Jill felt a little sick. It was Mother he referred to, Mother he was blaming. But before she could say anything in Mother's defense, or her own, Adrian gathered the broken bits of the vase into his hands and stalked off to the room he shared with Andy, slamming the door behind him.

When Andy came home, bringing a new pane of glass for the bedroom window, and set to work putting it in, he wanted to know what Jill was upset about. But somehow she couldn't tell him.

6

POSTMAN'S ERROR

ONE morning a week or so after the disaster of the vase, Jill looked out the window to see the Chinese postman coming up the walk. She ran out for the mail and then took the letters to Mother who was upstairs vacuuming the bedroom.

Mother liked to get mail from her friends in New York and she shut off the motor and took the envelopes, running through them quickly to see who had written to her.

" Here's one that's not ours," she said. " Your friend the postman has left us a letter that belongs to the house up the hill. Mm — it looks as though the lady really is a baroness."

Jill looked at the envelope her mother held. The typewritten address read: " Baroness Lydia von Wallenstein." The return address showed the printed stationery of a museum halfway across the country.

" Here's your chance," said Mother. " You might as well take this right up the hill. Then you can ask whoever comes to the door if Hana may visit you sometime soon."

After what she had heard about Miss Furness, Jill wasn't sure she would have the courage to offer such an invitation. Somewhat doubtfully she walked up the road to the house above.

The rear passageway opened to the street on which the Dallas house fronted, but the main entrance of the big house was on the road that ran along the hilltop. Once or twice Jill had climbed the hill and walked past the house, studying it curiously. But she had never ventured near the long flight of stone steps to the front entrance.

Stone walls, topped by a spiked iron fence, ran around the property. But while fences and gates separated the gardens on either side of the steps, the steps themselves were unbarred and ran steeply up to the front door, pausing only once at a landing. The house was three stories high, if you counted the dormer floor with its towers. The windows were shuttered and dark and no sign of life stirred anywhere. The big double front door was of heavy, ornately carved wood and it had a forbidding look. As she mounted the steps Jill began to feel small and very timid.

When she put her finger to the bell, she could hear the shrill summons go echoing through the house. Then all was still again and Jill waited uneasily. She was almost ready to give up and retreat when she heard the faint sound of someone approaching the door. The steps came lightly, swiftly, on a run, and the door was opened a crack. But it was only Hana Tamura who looked out at her inquiringly.

Jill put the letter behind her back. Now that she

had come so far, she wanted to give it into the hands of
the baroness herself, if possible. Perhaps she would give
permission for Hana to come to visit, even if the stern
Miss Furness would not.

" Prease? " said Hana, changing " l " to " r " as she
often did.

Jill smiled at her. " Hello. I wonder if I could see
the — the baroness? I — have a message for her."

Hana looked both baffled and helpless, as if she had
no notion of what to say or do. Before she could find
words to answer Jill, a cold voice spoke suddenly from
the garden beside the steps: " What do you want, little
girl? "

Jill turned quickly. The woman stood behind the
iron gate at the side, but she did not open it. She was
tall and thin, with a high-bridged nose and thin, tight
lips that had surely never seen lipstick. She was gowned
completely in black and the skirt of her old-fashioned
dress came nearly to her ankles. Unlike the lady of the
tower, this woman's hair was not a beautiful bright
silver that fluffed about her face, but rusty iron gray,
drawn tightly back from her forehead into a wispy bun
at the back of her head. All the lines of her face seemed
to drop unhappily downward and she looked as if she
hadn't smiled in years.

Hana closed the door softly and quickly without a
word, and Jill went slowly down the steps to the gate.
This, she knew, was Miss Furness, the person who
seemed to run things in this house and who had made
such stern rules for Hana.

Jill handed the letter through the spiked bars of the

gate. " The postman made a mistake and left this at
our house. My mother asked me to bring it to you."

Miss Furness said, " Thank you," curtly, took the
letter and walked off into the garden without a further
glance at Jill. She moved so quickly that there was no
chance to ask about Hana, no chance to get into any
sort of conversation. Jill had been thanked and dismissed all in one breath. Helplessly she stared after
the woman who seemed to have forgotten her. All
Miss Furness' interest was bent upon the letter in her
hands. As Jill watched, she ripped it open with a fore-
finger and removed the letter from the envelope. This
in itself seemed to Jill a shocking thing to do. At home
Mother had always taught her to respect mail addressed
to other people. Mother would never have opened one
of her daughters' letters, or anything not addressed
to her.

A soft sound behind her made Jill turn to look up at
the dark double door of the house. One side of the door
was opening again, very softly and secretly, just a crack.
Since Miss Furness was paying no further attention,
Jill went curiously back up the steps. Perhaps Hana
had something to say to her after all. But it was not
Hana's voice which addressed her through the crack.
It was an elderly voice, rather high and quavery.

" Please come back tomorrow morning," the voice
said. " Tomorrow morning at ten o'clock. *Please*
come."

As Jill stared in blank astonishment, the door closed
as softly as it had opened. Everything was so quiet that
she felt she might have dreamed the sound of a voice,

if it hadn't been for the entreaty of the " please " which still echoed in her ears.

" Well? " said the other voice from the garden. " I thought you'd gone, little girl. Is there anything else you want? " Miss Furness had returned to the barred gate and was staring at her in disapproval.

Jill went guiltily down the steps. She could only hope that Miss Furness had not heard that soft whisper. The woman stood at the gate waiting, and Jill saw a corner of the letter sticking from the patch pocket in her skirt. As she waited for Jill her fingers were carefully tearing the envelope into bits. How queer — to keep the letter, but tear up the envelope from the museum. But the woman had asked her a question, and this was Jill's chance.

" Yes," Jill said, licking her tongue quickly over dry lips. " I — my mother that is — I mean we would like to invite Hana Tamura to come down to visit us."

" Hana! " Miss Furness echoed. " How do you happen to know Hana? "

Since an explanation would involve betrayal of the window breaker, Jill did not answer directly. " My mother said to ask you if she might come to see us," she repeated.

" And then," said Miss Furness, " I suppose you would want to come up here to see Hana? No, I'm afraid that wouldn't do at all. I prefer not to have her running around to visit neighbors. She has her own friends who live in another part of town."

Jill began to feel indignant, and some of her courage returned. " We wouldn't have to visit her," she said quickly. " We'd just like Hana to — "

" I have said she may not," Miss Furness snapped.
" No argument is necessary. My sister is not well. She
has been an invalid for many years and she cannot
stand noisy children laughing and playing close at
hand. As it is, we can hear you much too clearly from
down below."

This seemed a strange thing to say, considering the
interest the woman with silver hair had shown in what
was going on downhill, to say nothing of the odd invitation she had just issued to Jill.

" If you mean the baroness — " Jill began.

The woman's pale gray eyes regarded her chillingly.
" I mean my sister, Mrs. Wallenstein." Miss Furness
turned and walked through the side garden, disap-
pearing around the house.

There was nothing for Jill to do but go home. On
the way she puzzled over the queer things that had
happened. At least there was one thing Jill knew that
she had not known before. Miss Furness and the other
woman were sisters. But what an unkind way to treat
a sister!

She suspected that she ought to tell Mother all about
what had happened, but she had an uncomfortable feeling that Mother would say no to that odd, whispered
invitation and not let her go back tomorrow at ten.

If Adrian had been more approachable, Jill might
have told him about her morning's adventure. But
Adrian had been remote and gloomy ever since the
incident of the broken vase. True, he had been using
his new " studio." He had pulled the screens around

to give him privacy and sometimes disappeared behind them for hours on end, while the odor of paint
and turpentine invaded the house. But while he was
gravely polite when he came out from behind the
screens, he was hardly sociable.

That night at dinner Mother mentioned the letter
which the postman had left by mistake.

" It really was addressed to a baroness," she told
Mr. Dallas. " So that part can't be make-believe. It
was for Baroness Lydia von Wallenstein from a museum in the Middle West. I know it's none of our
business, but I can't help being interested."

" I think I know the answer to the museum part,"
Mr. Dallas said. " Just a few days ago a man on the
paper was telling me that we'd moved next door to an
almost forgotten San Francisco *cause célèbre.*"

" What's that? " asked Carol.

" It means an affair much talked about and publi-
cized — a celebrated cause. This fellow wasn't up on
the details, but he believes the Furness house is full
of valuable Oriental treasures and art objects. Stuff
brought back from Japan and China by Mrs. Wallenstein — or the baroness, if you prefer."

Adrian looked interested. " Oriental things? Wish I
could see them. Did your friend say why those two
shut themselves up the way they do? "

" He didn't know. But he says every once in a while
some museum digs up the story and tries to get hold
of the articles. There was some mystery years ago about
the death of Mrs. Wallenstein's husband — when she
first came to this country."

" But she's American," Jill said. She had not meant to blurt out her information, but now that she had done so she went on. " Miss Furness is her sister. And ' Miss Furness ' certainly sounds American. So the baroness must be too."

Mr. Dallas smiled at her. " Looks like you're the detective in the family, Jill. If you get a story out of it, let me know."

As they were finishing dessert, Mr. Dallas suggested that they all go downtown to see a movie which had just opened at a Market Street theater. Carol found that a wonderful idea, and Mother said cheerfully that she wanted to go. Jill did too, but before she could say so, Adrian shook his head.

" No, thanks, Dad," he said a little stiffly. " I've some work I want to finish tonight."

" All right," his father said, " Andy can come with us," and he looked at his other son.

Somewhat to Jill's surprise, Andy hesitated a moment and then shook his head. " I — I guess not. I'll stay home with Adrian."

" You needn't," said Adrian coolly.

Andy paid no attention. " I want to work on my stamp album," he said, but Jill knew quite clearly that he had chosen to stay home only because of Adrian.

Mr. Dallas was disappointed, but still cheerful. " At least we can count on you, Jill? "

Everyone stared at her except Adrian, who was plainly not interested in what she did. And suddenly Jill had the queer feeling that the choice she made was more important than it seemed. Whether the grownups felt it or not, the family had broken into two segments. On one side were the Spencers and Roger Dallas, on the other side Adrian and Andy, standing together against them. It was as if they were saying to their father, " Go ahead with them, but we two will stick together."

All this went through Jill's head in a flash and she had the strong feeling that there was only one way to break the line of division that was being drawn.

" I've got a stamp album too," she told the others. " So if Andy is going to work on his, I'll get mine out and maybe we can trade stamps."

Jill felt sorry to disappoint Mother. She wished she could say, " I do want to see that movie, but somebody's got to step over the line so they can't be against us."

" Perhaps," Mr. Dallas said, " this is the wrong night to suggest a movie and — "

Mother didn't let him finish. " I don't think we should change our plans because the children don't want to go. You and Carol and I can have a lovely time." She glanced at her watch and Jill spoke quickly.

" I'll do the dishes. Then you can catch the early show."

That was the way they worked it out. Just before she left, Mother came out to the kitchen to give Jill a quick squeeze.

" I think I understand, honey," she said. " See if you can break up that two-against-the-world club while we're gone. Oh dear, I do wish I knew how to make friends with Adrian."

Jill wished the same thing as she washed dishes and dried them, without any help from the boys. She had begun to dry glasses when a couple of faint " pings " sounded in the living room. Neither radio nor television was on. Someone had struck two notes on the long unopened piano. Jill tiptoed to the door and looked into the living room. There was Adrian sitting at the piano, his back to her. He was moving his hands gently over the keys as if he played a sound-less melody. Nearby Andy sat on the floor beside the coffee table, with his album open and stamps spread out around it. But he was not looking at the stamps. His attention was fixed on his brother.

" Go ahead and play something," Andy said, sound-ing a little gruff, as if this meant more than he wanted his brother to guess.

By way of answer, Adrian closed the piano with a thud. " I don't feel like it." He sat on the piano bench staring into space, while Andy fiddled absently with his stamps.

Remembering the interest Adrian had shown at the idea of Oriental treasures up in the Furness house, Jill decided to tell what she had been holding back. Maybe this was something to interest the boys and break that uncomfortable silence.

" I think I'll go up to see the baroness tomorrow morning," she announced, her voice sounding louder than she intended.

Adrian swung about on the bench and Andy put down his tweezers and magnifying glass. For once Jill certainly had their attention. She gave the glass in her hands an energetic polishing.

" I've been invited to come up to visit her tomorrow morning," she said, trying to sound matter-of-fact.

" You're making it up," said Adrian. " Miss Furness would never — "

" Not Miss Furness. The baroness."

" You mean you talked to her? " Andy demanded.

" Not exactly. After Miss Furness took the letter, the other lady opened the door a crack and asked me to please come up to the house tomorrow at ten o'clock. Then she closed the door and that was all. I don't know whether to go or not."

Andy pointed out that it seemed rather sensible for Mrs. Wallenstein to pick the time of day when her sister went down the hill to shop and took Mr. Tamura with her.

Adrian shrugged. " Why don't you tell Jill about that time she threw a stone at us? Anyway, Jill wouldn't have the nerve to go up there, even if Dad does think she's such a good detective."

" I'm not afraid to go up there tomorrow," Jill said quickly.

Adrian grinned and she knew he didn't believe her. She was sorry now that she had followed her impulse to stay home with the two boys. A movie would have been fun. But at the same time she knew that the atmosphere was different because she had stayed. If she had gone the two boys might have been commiserating with each other by now and siding against Mother. At least she had stopped that for the time being.

She returned to the kitchen and Adrian went to work

again behind his screens. Andy had rigged him up a good bright light for his studio section.

While Jill was putting things away, Andy came out to the kitchen and laid something on the edge of the sink. Jill picked up what looked like another bit of stone from the crumbling wall, but this piece was only a pebble, too small to do any harm.

" Is this the stone Adrian keeps talking about? " she asked.

Andy nodded. " She didn't throw it to hurt anyone. It was wrapped in a piece of paper. A note. I didn't show it to Adrian because I don't feel like sneering at that old lady. I have a feeling that she'd like to have friends and that her sister keeps everyone away from her for some reason."

" Did you keep the note? " Jill asked.

Andy took a crumpled bit of paper from his pocket and smoothed it out. Words were penciled across it in wavery handwriting. Jill held the paper up to the light, but she could barely make out the writing.

The words read: *Please help me find my little green cat.*

That was all. And how very queer! Suddenly Jill didn't want to go back to that old house and see the woman who had written this.

" Are you really going to see her tomorrow? " Andy asked, watching Jill's expression.

" I — I don't know," she had to admit.

" If you do," said Andy calmly, " I'd like to go with you."

Jill stared at him for a moment. Then she nodded. Unexpectedly she had found an " accomplice." She wouldn't mind visiting the baroness if Andy came along.

7

MISS LYDIA

THE next morning was an especially foggy one. Fortunately Mother had planned to take Carol to her first San Francisco dancing lesson. They left the house before nine thirty and Jill and Andy each breathed a sigh of relief. Adrian, of course, was off to his own class and they had not told him their plans.

Jill watched the clock, and at three minutes to ten she and Andy walked up the hill together. Now that Andy was along, this seemed more like an adventure and she was only a little uneasy.

Nevertheless, Jill wished there had been sunshine on this particular morning. Fog drifted through the streets of San Francisco, so that every road looked wavery and mysterious, and even ordinary houses took on a ghostly aspect. The Furness house looked queerer than ever, with its towers pointing eerily through the mist.

" Do you think we've waited long enough? " Jill asked anxiously as they climbed the hill. " What if we run into Miss Furness? "

" We won't." Andy was confident. " We could set a clock by most of the things she does. On marketing day she always leaves at ten minutes to ten. I've seen her lots of times. So we've already missed her by ten minutes. And she'll be gone for more than an hour. They don't have a car and she and Mr. Tamura always walk."

The house was hushed and still as they climbed the long stone steps. But this time, before Jill could put her finger to the doorbell, the door opened wide upon a dimly lighted hallway. For just a second there appeared to be no one in the hall. Then Hana put her head around the edge of the door, finger to lips, and beckoned them in.

" Prease to keep still," she whispered. " We do not tell my mother."

Faint light from outdoors seeped through a colored glass window high on one wall, and a lamp bulb burned dimly at the far end of the wide hall. Outside the world of fog was shadowless, but here shadows were thick in every corner; they reached to envelop the visitor. The hall itself was wide and long. A wooden balcony railing ran completely around it at the second-story level, and Jill was aware of dark stairs mounting into the gloom, and of another set of double doors at the far end that seemed to duplicate the front doors.

Hana moved lightly ahead of them, a small brave inhabitant of this gloomy world, and they had to follow her quickly or lose her. She led them to a door at one side of the hall and when she opened it daylight streaked in welcome toward them. They stepped into a big room furnished in a rather odd manner.

The mantelpiece was marble, with a little marble cupid sitting in the middle of it, aiming his arrow at the high ceiling. The great mirror that rose behind him had a gilt curlicue frame. Against one wall stood a marble-topped table with a lamp on it. There were knickknack shelves in the corners, and a high bookcase of dark reddish wood. But the odd thing was that all the furniture seemed to have been pushed back against the walls — there were only a couple of chairs — and the floor was completely bare of a rug.

Hana hurried toward a rear door hung with a curtain of bamboo beads and spoke softly. " Miss Rydia! Company is now here."

" Rydia " would of course mean Lydia, Jill thought. Though Hana tried to correct her " l " sounds, they often came out wrong. There was an unidentifiable sound from the next room and Jill glanced at Andy. He looked solemn, but not uneasy. She was glad to have him with her this morning. Andy would not be easily alarmed, no matter what happened.

Hana held the rustling curtains aside and a silver-haired old lady in a modern wheel chair came through the door. She was the prettiest old lady Jill had ever seen. Her cheeks were faintly wrinkled, but they wore the youthful pink of excitement, as if she had looked forward to the arrival of company with the interest of a child. Her eyes were a bright dancing blue and her smile revealed how very lovely she must have been as a girl. Unlike her sister, she did not dress in black, but wore a frock of mossy green that set off her silver hair.

It might have been the tea gown of another day and it draped softly from her waist to the tips of green satin slippers that showed their toes beneath its hem.

The little chair was all chrome and rubber and Mrs. Wallenstein had remarkable control of it. She did not wait for Hana to push her forward, but wheeled the chair speedily toward Jill and Andy. When she came to a halt before them she held out a hand to each in turn.

" How nice that you've really come," she said in the high, faintly wavery voice that Jill remembered. " Do bring those chairs out from the wall and sit down. I try to keep the room uncluttered so I can get about easily. First of all I want to know your names."

It was Jill who introduced herself and Andy, while he brought the chairs. Hana hovered nearby and Mrs. Wallenstein smiled and spoke to her in what must be Japanese. The girl laughed and bowed to her before running out of the room.

" Even though this is the middle of the morning," Mrs. Wallenstein said, " we are going to have a tea party. I hope you won't mind pretending that it's four in the afternoon. My sister Matilda seldom leaves the house in the late afternoon, so this is the only tea party I can manage."

Neither Jill nor Andy had the faintest notion what to say and, since their hostess seemed quite happy to chatter, their lack of words didn't make any difference.

" Of course you don't know anything about me," Mrs. Wallenstein ran on, " but I feel that I know you quite well, considering that you've occupied the house below us for such a short while. In fact, I know a great deal more about the people in all the houses down the hill than they'd ever expect, just by watching them with my glasses. Do you suppose people are annoyed with me? It worries Matilda. Now and then she hides my glasses, but Hana always finds them for me. Hana is my friend and aide in this house. She has better sense than to regard me as an invalid."

Jill stole a sidelong glance at Andy to see how he was taking this rush of words. There was a faint smile on his wide mouth, as if he liked Mrs. Wallenstein, and Jill was relieved. Even though she couldn't think of anything to say, she was ready to take sides even more strongly than before against Miss Matilda Furness.

Hana came back quickly. She must have had this tray already prepared in the kitchen and had only to pour the water for the tea. It was a beautiful tray of black and gold lacquer, with a green-flowered Japanese tea set upon it and thin cookies of a pale gold color on a flowered plate. A sprig of blossoms from the garden added a decorative touch of pink and dark green.

The handle of the teapot was of curved bamboo, but the small cups had no handles. Mrs. Wallenstein poured each one a cup of pale green tea and told them they must drink it in the Japanese manner, without sugar or cream. The little cookies were real *sembi,* she said — rice cakes from Japan.

Hana sat on a footstool near Mrs. Wallenstein's chair, drinking tea and plainly enjoying the party. Jill didn't care much for tea and she suspected Andy would have preferred milk, but they both sipped politely, nibbled and listened.

" Is Mama-san still doing the laundry? " Mrs. Wallenstein asked Hana.

Hana's black eyes danced as she nodded. " I am most disobedient daughter," she admitted happily.

Mrs. Wallenstein reached out a frail hand with a long jade ring upon it and patted Hana's arm. " I don't know what I'd do without Hana. But now perhaps you two young people will visit me occasionally when my sister is out. We'll keep our little secret as long as we can."

Jill was increasingly curious to know why this pleasant old lady should be practically imprisoned here by her sister, and now her mounting curiosity got the better of her.

" Mrs. Wallenstein, why doesn't your sister want you to have company? " she asked.

The silvery head moved gently from side to side. " You mustn't blame Matilda. She means well. I was seriously ill for a long time and she tried to keep my life quiet and without excitement. She is devoted to me, but she is also entirely mistaken about what is good for me now. Since she is a very strong-minded woman — and I am tied to this chair — there is little I can do about it. She permits old friends to visit me, but I'm sure she warns them not to talk of subjects which might excite me. She treats me like an old woman, just because I am seventy, though she is two years older than I am. Sometimes I feel more than two years younger than Matilda! "

Jill had to ask the next question that was tantalizing her. " Are you really a baroness? "

Hana sat up on her footstool and looked suddenly anxious. For just a moment a puzzled look clouded Mrs. Wallenstein's bright gaze. She repeated the word rather doubtfully.

" A baroness? We don't have such things in America, do we? Yes — I believe I was a baroness long ago. Certainly Karl was a baron. But he was never one for staying at home in Austria to live up to his title."

Hana left her stool and ran to a big window at the side of the house, as if to create a distraction. " The fog goes away! " she announced. " Mah! sun is coming out! "

" That's nice," said Mrs. Wallenstein cheerfully. " I like to sit in my tower room when it's clear and watch the lives of all the people on the hill. But I like the fog too. It makes everything look different — mysterious and interesting."

" Have more *sembi*," said Hana, coming back to pass the plate of rice cakes again. She was behaving in such an odd nervous way that Jill suspected she was trying to get the talk away from the baron.

Mrs. Wallenstein remained undisturbed. " You really mustn't call me by such a long name as Wallenstein," she said. " Hana has a name for me that I like. Will you two call me ' Miss Lydia ' also? "

" Sure, Miss Lydia," Andy said, grinning a little self-consciously, and Jill nodded.

" Fine! Now you must tell me about the other boy and the little girl who live in the house with you. I've been trying to figure out the relationship. You don't seem exactly like sisters and brothers."

This was a safe enough topic. Jill explained readily, while Miss Lydia listened in delight. Seldom had Jill had such an interested audience. The first thing she knew she was talking about Carol's dancing and Adrian's painting — which led easily to another question. A question she wanted to ask for Adrian's sake.

"We've heard that you used to live in Japan," Jill said, "and that you brought home things from the Orient. Andy's brother, Adrian, is especially interested in Japanese and Chinese art. He has been wishing he could see some of your things."

Hana squirmed again on her stool and Jill wondered what she had said now that was wrong.

Once more Miss Lydia looked faintly puzzled. "That's quite right," she said, as if this were a subject she had not considered for a long while. "Karl and I always planned that when we were older we would build a house in San Francisco and furnish it with treasures from the Orient. There were always things we couldn't bear to let the museums have, you know. My husband was an explorer and very well known. He often made expeditions for the world's museums, and he was a collector in his own right. When we lived in Japan our little house was fairly a museum in itself. Hana — what do you suppose Matilda has done with all Karl's treasures?"

Hana looked almost frightened. She shook her head helplessly. There were no more *sembi* to pass and the tea was finished. She threw a pleading look at Jill, and though Jill didn't know what was the matter she tried to help.

" I wish you could see my sister Carol dance," she said, this being the only change of subject she could think of.

Miss Lydia seemed not to hear the distraction. " Karl was lost on his last expedition in China. A sad loss for the world, as well as tragic for me. He brought so much that was beautiful out of places where it was hidden, discovered so much about little-known peoples." She pressed her fingers against her temples, as if trying to think more clearly. " Yes — it was only last year that he was lost and I — " her voice broke and the words halted.

Hana spoke quickly to Jill. " More better you go now. Soon Miss Furness comes."

Both Andy and Jill said good-by and tried to thank Miss Lydia for the party, but she seemed scarcely to hear them. Her words ran on and her voice was more wavery than ever.

" It was a dangerous expedition — into bandit territory. I can't remember. . . . I can't remember. . . . If only I could find my little cat! My little green cat." She looked at the children intently. " That's it — that's why I asked you here! Someone has to help me. Hana can't and Matilda won't. Someone must help me find my little green cat."

This was too much for Jill. Poor Miss Lydia's memory was clearly wandering and the quicker they left, the better. She and Andy hurried from the room and Hana took them into the wide, bewildering hall and led them to the front door.

" Poor lady," Hana said sadly. " Is almost thirty-five

years that husband is lost in China. It is better she forgets. She is in mos' bad happening in Japan before she comes to this country."

"We didn't know," Jill said. "We must have said everything wrong. But what does she mean about a green cat?"

Hana merely shook her head, helpless to answer the question. So Jill tried a more personal one. "Hana, have you asked Miss Furness if you can visit us?"

"Yes, I have not asked," said Hana, nodding her head, so that Jill felt more confused than ever. "Is no good to ask."

"Well, I'm not going to give up," Jill told her. "Perhaps Mother will write her a note sometime and invite you to our house. Just because she has to keep her sister a prisoner —"

"Oh, come now!" said a gay voice behind them. "I'm not really a prisoner, you know."

Miss Lydia had propelled her chair over the doorsill and into the hall and was rolling toward them quickly. In the light from the open front door Jill saw that the vague expression was gone from her eyes and she looked quite cheerful and untouched by tragedy.

"You mustn't get the wrong idea, my dears. It is true that I am not very strong. But I know that I can do more than Matilda thinks I should. Life would be more interesting if I could prove that to her. I've always been fond of children, though we had none of our own. It will help a great deal if you'll come to see me again. Will you, Jill? Will you, Andy? And bring the little sister who dances and the brother who paints!"

She was so winning, so eager, so charming, that Jill could only assure her that they would certainly try.

"That's a promise!" cried Miss Lydia, who seemed to have forgotten all about the green cat. "I'll send Hana down to let you know the very next time I'm alone —" She broke off and a listening look came into her face. "Do you hear something, children? What is that?"

"Is nothing," Hana said quickly. "Only fog horn out on bay."

Startled, Jill listened too, but to her ears the sounds meant only that the fog had not yet cleared from the water.

"That's right," Andy agreed. "Those are only whistles and horns from the bay."

But Miss Lydia shook her head. "No — it's a bell! I can hear it quite clearly. A temple bell, I think. Every now and then I seem to hear it and I always have a feeling that it's trying to tell me something. Something I should remember. But what its message is, I don't know."

Hana put small hands on the rear handles that propelled the wheel chair and turned it about. With a little nod of her head at Andy and Jill she plainly asked them to leave. Jill went out into the brightening day and Andy pulled the heavy door shut behind them.

They ran down the long flight of steps, eager to regain the everyday feeling of San Francisco streets and be away from that queer house and the old lady with the faulty memory. Once more on the sidewalk, Andy seemed to brace himself against the sense of panic

both he and Jill had felt for a few seconds in getting
away from the house.

" Goodness! " Jill said and drew a deep breath in relief. " I'm awfully glad you were with me. I'd have
been scared to pieces alone. I don't think I want to
go back. Do you? "

Andy, as she was beginning to learn, seldom made
quick decisions. He liked to think about something for
a while before he made up his mind.

" I don't know," he said. " Miss Lydia's nice when
she isn't getting mixed up about things that happened
a long time ago."

" I know," Jill agreed. " And I feel sorry for her —
shut up in that house without anything interesting to
occupy her. I'd hate it like anything. But at the same
time — "

Andy nudged her. " Ssh! " he said. " Look! "

Jill looked and caught her breath. Coming along the
hill road on the opposite side of the street was the tall,
bleak Miss Matilda Furness. Today an old-fashioned
hat, trimmed with rusty-black silk rosettes, was set
squarely upon her head and she marched down the
street with the air of a commander leading armies. Her
forces, however, were rather light. Following her was a
single figure, carrying a bag of groceries so high that
he had to peer around behind it. This must be Mr.
Tamura, Hana's father.

Under her breath Jill whispered to Andy. " Do you
think she saw us come down the steps? "

" I don't know," he muttered. When they came
abreast of the two across the street, he looked straight

at Miss Lydia's sister and grinned. " Good morning, Miss Furness," he said cheerfully.

She looked at them suspiciously and replied with a grudging good morning. But she said nothing more as she crossed the street to her house. Behind her Mr. Tamura peered around his tall paper bag and smiled at them in a friendly fashion. He did not speak, but as he went by he gave them a quick little nod of his head, and both Andy and Jill smiled back at him.

At least Mr. Tamura was ready to be friends, even if Miss Furness was not. Probably Hana had told him about her visit to the Dallas house and how she had been received.

" I'd hate to be up there now and get caught by Miss Furness," Jill said as they turned the corner at their own street.

" What could she do except ask you to leave? " Andy asked.

Probably that was true, but just the same Jill felt relieved that they had missed her and would not have to face her anger.

8

ADRIAN THE CRITIC

THAT afternoon several boys came to the
house for Andy. Mother did her best to
make them welcome, but they had some sort of boy
project lined up and took Andy off with them. Adrian's friends never came to the house, and there didn't
seem to be many of them. He was a dreamy sort of boy
who was not unhappy keeping to himself. But this afternoon he went out too, visiting somebody in his old
neighborhood.

He didn't exactly tell Mother where he was going.
He just announced it to the air in the living room. He
seemed to be pretending that Mother wasn't there at
all. Only when it was necessary did he address her directly and even then he didn't look at her. If he glanced
in her direction he seemed to look through her as if
she were air. When he mentioned where he was going
he apparently did so only because of orders his father
had given earlier.

Carol had found a little girl her own age in a house
across the street, and the two were on the rear terrace
with their dolls. Mother sat at the red-and-chrome table
in the kitchen with a cookbook open before her, while

Jill perched on the kitchen stool and watched her turn the pages. She wished she could relate the whole story of the visit she and Andy had made to the house on the hill, but she wasn't quite ready for that. Perhaps she would tell Mother tomorrow.

Right now she was mainly angry with Adrian. After all, she and Mother had done their best to please him and make friends with him.

Mother glanced at her and seemed to know what lay behind her expression. " Don't be impatient with Adrian, Jill. We'll just have to give him more time. I'm sure he needs our affection, but he thinks right now that the only sort of love he wants is what he could get from his mother. We'll have to show him that we can think a lot of him and appreciate him too. Not in the way of taking his mother's place, but in our own way."

Jill said, " Mmph! Did you see the way he acted at lunch? He pretended you weren't even there. I thought he'd put a hand right through you a couple of times as if you were nothing."

Mother looked a little sad, but not angry. "It's his way of trying to be loyal to his mother, Jill. I suspect he has the foolish notion that if he should get to like us — especially me — he would be forgetting his mother. Of course it isn't true, but I don't know how to make him see that."

She turned back to the pages of the cookbook and Jill came to look over her shoulder.

" This is a collection of foreign recipes," Mother said. " I found it in a carton of books Roger brought from the other house. Look — doesn't this seem interesting? "

She rested her finger on a color photograph that looked like pieces of meat stuck on a long spike.

" It's called 'shish kebab,' " Mother said. " It's an Armenian dish made with hunks of lamb and bits of mushrooms, eggplant, and tomato alternating on a skewer. Don't you think it sounds like the sort of thing boys would like? And it doesn't seem hard to make."

Jill looked at the picture doubtfully. She knew these signs from long experience. Nothing ever looked hard in print to Mother. But when it came to making the dish the queerest things went wrong.

" Maybe you could practice it a few times when Adrian and Andy aren't here," Jill suggested.

Mother nodded, her eyes dancing. " A good idea, honey. I'll pick days when the boys are away at lunchtime and make it just for us."

She tore a slip of paper from a scratch-pad and slipped it between the pages to mark the place. Then she replaced the book in the kitchen drawer.

" Jill, I want to tell you — last night Roger made a plan for the four of you. We feel that an outing in which you could go off together and leave us grownups at home would be a good idea. It will help a lot if Adrian begins to like you and Carol."

Jill wasn't too sure about this plan. Her doubts about Adrian were increasing. But she waited for her mother to explain further.

" We thought you might take a trip to the Coit Tower," Mother said. " Next Sunday would be a good

time. That's a few days off, so Adrian can get used to
the idea."

Adrian, Mother pointed out, knew all about the
tower and the woman it had been named for. Jill could
ask questions and let Adrian have the fun of telling
them all about it. The view up there would be wonderful on a clear day and it would be an interesting
way to get to know more about San Francisco.

Because of Adrian, Jill still felt uneasy. However,
she wanted to go up the tower, and if there could just
be another girl along — someone older and more sensible than Carol —

A sudden idea struck her. " Mother, do you suppose
we could invite Hana Tamura to go with us? "

Mother wasn't a bit like Andy. She had a way of
zooming right up to a question and making up her
mind about it in a split second. As she sometimes admitted, the result wasn't always the best possible
choice, but at least it made things happen fairly
quickly.

" I don't know why not! " she said, getting up from
the table. " In fact, I think it's a very good idea. I'll
make a phone call right now and invite her."

Jill trailed after her mother into the living room,
worried at this sudden speed. " But Miss Furness — I
mean, she said — "

Mother was looking up the number. " I won't talk to
Miss Furness. Not first anyway." She sat down cheerfully and dialed the number, while Jill held her breath.

" Hello? . . . I'd like to speak to Mr. Tamura,
please."

Mother put her hand over the phone and looked at Jill, her eyes ashine with mischief.

" That was Hana. A break for our side. I might have had trouble with one of the old ladies."

Not with Miss Lydia, Jill thought. But then, Miss Lydia wouldn't answer the telephone.

In a moment Jill heard the sound of a voice in the receiver and Mother spoke into the mouthpiece again.

" Good afternoon, Mr. Tamura. This is Mrs. Dallas . . . from the house below you. We were so pleased to meet your daughter Hana the other day. Now we're wondering if she would care to go with our children to the Coit Tower next Sunday? . . . That's right. . . . Jill is new in this neighborhood, you know, and she would like to know Hana better. . . . Thank you, Mr. Tamura, that's fine. We'll look for her around eleven thirty. . . . Good-by."

She set down the phone and dusted her hands with an air of accomplishment.

" You mean he said yes? " Jill asked in astonishment.

" Of course he did. It was easy as pie. He is probably a sensible man who wants his daughter to be happy and have friends. He certainly isn't living in a feudal country where an employer can make such impossible rules. Miss Furness can say she doesn't want children up there, but she can't — "

Jill winced, remembering how recently she had been up there. Mother broke off and looked at her closely for a moment. Then she went on.

" Miss Furness can't prevent Hana from going out with you if her father gives his permission."

Partly because she was pleased over this unexpected turn, and partly to escape her mother's penetrating look, Jill took a whirl about the room. But she was less graceful than Carol, and knocked over a magazine rack. By the time everything was straight again, Mother seemed to have forgotten her moment of suspicion and had thought of something else.

" Jill, dear," she said, and her daughter recognized a coaxing note in her voice that meant something difficult was coming.

Jill said nothing, waiting.

Mother looked wistful. " Roger and I wish you could stop calling him ' Mr. Dallas.' It sounds so distant and stiff."

Jill knew she was flushing uncomfortably. It wasn't that she didn't want to do what they asked, but just that " Roger " did not come naturally to her, as it did to Carol. Whenever she thought of saying it out loud she got tongue-tied and self-conscious. But there was no way to explain this.

Mother recognized her distress. " All right, honey. It will come in time. I don't want to push you."

But Jill found herself wondering if she could ever manage to call her stepfather anything but " Mr. Dallas."

That night at dinner the trip to the Coit Tower made a topic for lively conversation. Even if Adrian held back, the others had things to say. Jill told about how Hana was going to join them, and Andy said he'd take his camera along and get some pictures. Carol always loved anything that had the word " go " in it and

she, at least, never knew when anyone was trying to
snub her or hurt her feelings. So she had no reserva-
tions about the trip.

If it had not been for his father's eye upon him, Jill
suspected that Adrian might have tried to back out,
just on general principles. But Mr. Dallas looked as if
he might put his foot down in no uncertain way.
Plainly he was losing patience with his son, and Adrian
must have decided to avoid trouble on this occasion at
least. Though he was still pretending that Emily was
thin air, and even Mother was growing a little dis-
pleased over that. After dinner Adrian disappeared behind his screens and Jill was relieved to see him go.
Sir Galahad in blue jeans! she thought scornfully and
made a face at her own sentimental notion.

When Mr. Dallas went out to work for a while in the
garden that evening, Jill looked for Andy and saw that
he was in the bookcase corner of the living room. He
was pulling down old books one after another, and
riffling through the pages. Jill decided to go over and
see what he was searching for. But as she started across
the room, Carol, who lay on her stomach on the floor,
looking at a new magazine, started up with a yelp of
triumph.

" Adrian! " she cried. " Adrian, come here and look!
I want to show you what I've found in this magazine."

So far Adrian had never been unkind to Carol. He
poked his head around a screen and Carol held up the
advertisement which had attracted her attention. Jill
saw that it was one of Mother's drawings. Mother had
a way of drawing cunning, dimpled children that made

other parents not only want to cuddle the toddlers in the pictures, but rush right out and dress their own children in similar styles. That was what made such a demand for her fashion drawings.

" Look, Adrian! " Carol rattled on. " My mother drew these. I told you what a good artist she is."

Mother came to the kitchen door, the pinkness of embarrassment in her cheeks. " Oh, Carol! " she murmured helplessly.

Jill hoped Adrian would just go back out of sight and never mind, but instead he came out with a paint-brush in one hand and knelt beside Carol to look at the fashion ad drawings.

The worst of it was he didn't say anything. Not anything at all. He just looked carefully at the entire lay-out in the most scornful way possible. Mother's cheeks grew pinker until Jill couldn't tell whether she was getting angry, or ready to cry. Something had to be done — though Jill wasn't sure what.

" They paid my mother a lot of money for those drawings," she announced stoutly. " Does anybody pay you for yours, Adrian Dallas? "

Adrian got slowly to his feet. It was hard to face him when he stood tall like that and looked down at her from his superior vantage point.

" That's not the way I'd want to earn money," Adrian said. Then politely — too politely — to Mother: " Did you ever have a chance to study draw-ing and painting? "

For just a minute Mother looked shocked at Adrian's brashness. She had, as Jill knew, worked very hard earning her way through a school in commercial art. Jill began to sputter, but Mother threw her a warning look that hushed her and answered Adrian with quiet dignity.

" I haven't studied nearly enough," she told him and went back to the kitchen.

Her unexpectedly gentle answer seemed to take the wind out of Adrian's sails. He stared after her uncomfortably and returned to his painting. Jill was still angry and it was probably just as well that Andy spoke to her just then.

" I've found something you might like to see," he said, holding out a book almost pleadingly.

She choked back her impulse to tell Adrian a few things and went to look at what Andy had found.

" I guess Dad forgot about this book too," he said. " It's one we had at the old house. Start reading here."

Jill took the book, looking first at the title. It was called *New Century in San Francisco* and had been published in 1903. As she began to read the paragraphs Andy had pointed out, her eyes fell upon the name " Furness."

She forgot about Adrian as her interest came to life. Curled up on the couch, she began to read.

9

JILL TAKES A WRONG TURN

As Jill read about the early days of the new century in San Francisco, a picture began to come clear in her mind. The Furness family, quite prominent in society, though not of the wealthy Nob Hill set, had lived in a fine house on Russian Hill. The house described was plainly the same house that still raised its pinnacles on the hill above.

Lydia Furness at seventeen must have been a very beautiful and vivacious girl, in fact, one of the most charming and lovely of San Francisco's beautiful girls. The feminine writer became a little flowery in her praises, but Jill, remembering the beauty that still shone in the face of silver-haired Miss Lydia, could well believe in her loveliness as a girl. The older sister, Matilda, was brushed somewhat carelessly aside, so she must not have been at all attractive.

Apparently there were suitors on every hand, even to foreign nobility, for Lydia's hand. Karl von Wallenstein, a young Austrian baron, was visiting the country in an effort to interest American museums in the expedition he planned on the far side of the world. He had lingered in San Francisco longer than he had intended because he was courting Lydia Furness. She had seemed to look upon him with favor and everyone was surprised when he suddenly went away.

Of course the reason might be the death of Lydia's mother and the long illness of her older sister. The girl apparently felt it her duty to stay at home with her father and her sister, Matilda, whom she must nurse in her need. But it seemed a pity, said the writer wistfully. Baron Karl was a handsome, dashing fellow, and European titles were all the rage these days with American girls. Karl had gone off to mysterious reaches of the Orient, and goodness knew what might become of him.

Carol yawned, closed her magazine and wandered outside to watch Mr. Dallas. Andy dropped down on the end of the couch near Jill.

" What do you think of it? " he asked.

Jill scanned a few more paragraphs, but this was apparently all the writer had to say about the Furness family.

" It's very romantic," Jill said.

Andy wrinkled his nose at so sissy a word. " Karl must have come back to San Francisco later, since she did marry him finally. But in the meantime she must have taken care of her sister the way Miss Furness is taking care of her now. Funny how things have turned out."

It was odd, too, Jill thought, that one of the sisters had been so beautiful and popular, and the other one so plain that no one had wanted to marry her. She said so, thinking out loud. Andy caught her up right away, sounding indignant.

" I expect it was her disposition nobody wanted to marry. My mother wasn't pretty, the way your mother is, but that didn't make any difference in the way Dad and Adrian and I loved her. She was always so kind and — and swell." He stopped with the sound of a break in his voice and Jill felt a surge of pity for him.

This was the first time Andy had really let his own feelings show and suddenly the barrier that stood between Mother and these two boys seemed hopelessly insurmountable. Andy too was resisting Mother, though he wasn't mean about it the way Adrian was.

" I didn't mean anything," Jill said awkwardly, " except that Miss Lydia is still pretty, even as an old lady."

Andy took the book back to the bookcase and after that he went outside too, and Jill felt somehow lonesome in this house full of people.

She was still feeling that way the next afternoon when she went idly out to the rear terrace. Fog was again shutting out the sun and wreaths of mist curled about the turrets of the Furness house, giving it a ghostly look. Andy was away, Carol was dancing, Adrian painting, and Jill wished she had someone her own age to visit with.

As if in answer to her wish Hana's head appeared suddenly over the lower wall. She flashed her quick, shy smile and waved, pointing toward the gate at the end of the passage.

Jill started through the house, almost bumping into her mother. She ducked past without explanation, noting that Mother had a sketch pad in her hands. At any other time she would have been interested, but right now she had to find out what Hana wanted.

She hurried out the front door and up the hill. Hana waited for her at the barred gate at the lower end of the passage. When Jill appeared, she pulled back the bolt and swung the gate open.

Quickly Jill stepped through into the narrow passageway that wound uphill between high walls. At once Hana swung the gate shut and bolted it, so that Jill had for a moment the queer feeling of being locked into a palace dungeon. Along the passageway ahead fog had gathered, making this entryway look more mysterious than ever.

"You come see Miss Rydia now," said Hana, and started at once up the curving passage.

Jill hurried after her. "Wait, Hana. I don't think I'd better go up there again. I mean — after all — " Part of the "after all" had to do with the fact that Andy wasn't along and that she felt nervous about facing that old house without him. It wasn't as though she lived there, as Hana did, and was accepted by Miss Matilda Furness.

Hana, however, was insistent. Miss Lydia had been looking forward to the next opportunity to see her recent visitors. Miss Furness had gone downtown on an unexpected errand, Mr. and Mrs. Tamura were busy upstairs in the house. This made a good opportunity to sneak Jill in to see Miss Lydia. Hana's loyalty to Miss Lydia gave her a single-minded purpose, and she didn't mean to take no for an answer.

There was an anxious moment at the top of the passageway where it opened into the back garden of the

Furness house. Hana, enjoying her conspirator's role, motioned Jill out of sight while she carefully scanned the upstairs windows of the house. Neither of the Tamuras was in sight, so Hana beckoned and both girls scuttled across the garden, running low as if they were playing Indians in ambush. Jill's heart was thumping when they reached the safety of the back door. She felt both uneasy and a little foolish.

In the gloom of the big old-fashioned kitchen, Hana moved like a small, dark-haired imp beside her.

" I am mos' disobedient Japanese daughter," she said, sounding pleased with herself. " Is fun to be like American daughter."

This was not the time, Jill felt, to explain that American daughters had better not be too disobedient or they got into trouble too. She was growing increasingly sure that Mother wouldn't approve of what she was doing and that sooner or later her actions would have to be explained at home. But now that she was in the middle of this curious adventure there was nothing to do but go ahead. Hana smuggled her through a narrow door into the big gloomy hall. A moment later she was in Miss Lydia's lighted sitting room and the little lady in the wheel chair was coming toward her eagerly.

" How nice that you could come, Jill," Miss Lydia said. " I hoped Hana could find one or the other of you. I'm sorry I can't give you a tea party today, but I'm not sure how long Matilda will be gone. We must be quiet so Hana's father and mother won't hear us. I'm afraid they might feel it necessary to report to Matilda." She chuckled, enjoying the conspiracy as Hana enjoyed it.

" Come over here and sit in my tower corner, Jill."

At least Miss Lydia seemed to be in a perfectly ra-
tional mood, and there was no talk about green cats or
of her husband, the baron.

" I'm sorry I was so stupid when you were here before," she said. " I knew I'd heard the name Dallas,
but it just didn't come to me until after you'd gone. Is
Andy's father the Roger Dallas who writes pieces for a
San Francisco paper? I'm sure he must be and I'm terribly pleased. I've been reading his articles for years.
I used to write a bit myself, you know. But I've lost all
touch with that sort of thing since my illness."

Jill said yes to her question about Mr. Dallas and let
her chatter on. Hana sat on a footstool nearby, her
hands clasped about blue-jeaned knees, a listening attitude upon her that was not wholly keyed to the conversation.

Today Miss Lydia wore a silver-gray dress that
matched her hair and again she looked pretty, with excitement brightening her eyes and cheeks. It really was
a shame, Jill thought, that she should be lonely and
hungry for company she could only entertain in secret.
Maybe the thing to do was confide in Mother and see if
they couldn't figure out a way to persuade Miss Furness
to put fewer restrictions upon her sister. The trouble
was, grownups were apt to feel they mustn't interfere.
They would probably consider Miss Matilda Furness'
wishes more than they would those of her invalid sister.

" So you see," Miss Lydia was running on, " I really
have done some writing in my time."

Jill's attention snapped back to what she was saying.

She had, she realized, missed quite a few words.

" So you see how interested I am," Miss Lydia said. " Please tell Mr. Dallas how much I enjoy his articles."

A sudden idea struck Jill and she sat upright on the padded tower seat. " Andy's father said just the other day that your old house ought to have a real story behind it. It might even be something he could write up if he could see the house and talk to you."

Miss Lydia's blue eyes twinkled. " What fun that would be! Though I'm afraid there really isn't any sort of story here. We never do anything except read and listen to the radio. My sister doesn't even approve of television. So what story he could find — "

" But there must be a story," Jill insisted, carried away by her idea. " What about that time when you were a young girl in San Francisco and Karl von Wallenstein wanted you to marry him? What happened after he went away and — "

The light went out of Miss Lydia's eyes and she shook her head quickly, paying no attention to Hana squirming uneasily on the footstool. " I had to send him away. My mother died suddenly, you know. And I had responsibilities to my father, and to my sister. Matilda was very ill at the time and someone had to care for her. Karl wanted to travel all over the world, so there wasn't anything else for me to do. But that doesn't make a very good story."

" He came back though — " Jill began.

Somewhere in the dim reaches of the house there was a creaking sound and Hana flew up from the stool as if a pin had pricked her. She clapped a small hand to each side of her head in a gesture of extreme despair.

" It is front door! " she wailed. " Miss Furness is come home! "

Miss Lydia straightened in her wheel chair and spoke kindly to Hana. " Never mind, child. Don't worry. The responsibility is mine. It's time I had a talk with Matilda about this nonsense of keeping me an invalid. Stay right where you are, Jill. I shall handle this."

But Miss Lydia clearly was no match for the woman who opened the door and stalked into the room, to stop with an amazed stare when she saw Jill on the window seat.

" Well! " she said. " And may I ask how you got in here? "

" This is Jill Spencer," Miss Lydia said, trying to keep the quaver out of her voice. " And I invited her to visit me. She is here as my guest. I hope she will come to see me many times in the future."

" Indeed, she'll do nothing of the sort," said Miss Furness. Her high-bridged nose looked like the sharp beak of an angry bird, and indignation was written all over her. " Hana, if you are to blame for this, I shall have to speak to your father."

Hana hung her head, plainly admitting the blame. Miss Furness hushed her sister, who was about to speak again, and pointed a thin finger at Jill.

" Go home, little girl. Go home at once. And don't ever come back here again! "

She was a frightening figure — tall and thin and iron gray. Jill couldn't say a word. As she went toward the door, she was aware that behind her Miss Lydia had burst into tears and that her sister was speaking to her soothingly in a low voice. Jill didn't wait for the frozen Hana to show her out. She stumbled into the dark confusion of the big hall and suddenly lost all sense of direction.

She hadn't the slightest idea which set of double doors led to the street. Both looked alike and she was turned about so that she didn't know which side the stairs should be on to find the front door. Blindly she chose and ran toward one set of doors. She was relieved when the knob moved in her hand and the door opened away from her. She slipped through, closing it behind — and knew that she had chosen the wrong way.

10

THE CURIO ROOM

This was not the foggy outdoors, but a big dark room that Jill had stepped into. At first she could scarcely make out the shadowy outlines. All the windows except a high one near the ceiling at the back had been covered by dark draperies and piled-up objects and furniture.

In the faint, misty light that seeped through from that one small window she could see that the room was so crowded with things dumped helter-skelter that one could hardly walk across it. It had a long-closed smell in which many odors mingled — dust, camphor, a whiff of stale incense, and other indefinable scents. Jill tried vainly to stifle a sneeze.

Her eyes were becoming accustomed to the dimness and she realized where she must be. This was the room in which Miss Matilda had evidently stored the art treasures Karl von Wallenstein had sent home from the Orient, intending to use them some day in his own home.

She must get out of the room quickly, before Miss Furness discovered the mistake she had made and became angrier than ever. But now that she was out of Miss Matilda's formidable presence, she felt increasingly curious about this room. What harm would there be in just looking around for a second or two? Miss Lydia had said there was no story in this house, but Jill was sure there must be. What an adventure to report to Adrian — if she ever decided to speak to him again. She could make his eyes pop with envy when she told him she had actually been inside the curio room.

Softly, softly, almost holding her breath, she moved into a narrow aisle on her left. All about her were queer, shadowy figures — there a snarling creature with a dog's body and a dragon's head; beyond a small, painted Buddha seated cross-legged with his fingers curled together in his lap.

She took another step and a hand grasped her sleeve so suddenly that she couldn't help a squeal of fright. But the hand belonged to the many-armed statue of a Hindu goddess and Jill's squeal changed to a nervous giggle. On down the aisle she went and around the corner of the room. As her eyes grew used to the gloom, the fearsome wonders about her became clear. Just as she drew near the uncluttered window, her toe struck something sticking sidewise into the aisle. Over her feet toppled a pile of books, making soft thudding sounds.

Books seemed odd to find in this room. One of them had fallen open and she could see the print in English on the page. She knelt to pick up the volumes and stack them back on the pile from which they had fallen. But, since she could never handle a book without looking at the title page to see what it was about, she paused in piling them up.

Into Ancient India was the title of this book and below in print were the words: *By Lydia von Wallenstein.*

Quickly Jill bent to read the titles and author's name on the spines of the other books in the stack. Every one of them had been written by that silver-haired old lady in the other room. Some were duplicates, but even at that there seemed to be at least ten titles. It was clear that Miss Lydia had made it her business to write up her husband's explorations into strange lands. Perhaps she had gone with him on many of his trips. The light was too dim to read the finer lettering in which the books were printed and Jill longed to take one of them home with her so she might read it through. That, however, was something she could hardly do without permission.

As she knelt there, holding a volume in her hands, she heard footsteps in the hall outside. Before she could stir someone opened the door into the curio room. Jill stayed where she was, kneeling out of sight behind piles of books and art objects. Whoever had opened the door remained quite still for a moment, then closed it with a firm pull. Jill's sigh of relief at not being caught was cut short by a new and dreadful sound.

Quite clearly she heard the turning of a key in the lock. Dropping the book from her fingers, Jill jumped to her feet. She couldn't be left a prisoner in this dismal place! But, even as she considered rushing to the door and pounding upon it, she held back. She didn't want

Miss Furness to discover her in this room. First she would see if there was any other way to get out.

After poking around for a few moments she realized that all the heaviest pieces had been pushed against the room's two main windows, shutting them off from easy access. There remained only that one high window through which pale light filtered into the room. For an instant panic rose in Jill. She hadn't minded the odd figures in which the room abounded, so long as she had only to walk away from them. But now an image with popeyes and lolling tongue seemed to leer at her evilly, and other queer creatures appeared to grimace. Suddenly it took a good deal of courage to walk past them.

She nerved herself for a dash and was relieved when she reached a place beneath the high window without having a red lacquered hand clutch her of its own volition.

It was dreadfully still in the room. The walls were probably thick and the doors heavy. She held her breath, hearing nothing at all from the rest of the house. It was as if she had stepped into another world. When something creaked eerily nearby, she jumped in terror. But all old houses creaked, she thought, trying to reassure herself.

She must get up on the carved chest beneath the little window and see if she could reach the latch. If she could open the window, she might be able to climb out through it. Then, if the drop to the ground wasn't too great, no one need be any the wiser about what she had done.

She turned her back on the popeyed fellow — afraid

that if she watched him for too long she would see that long tongue move — and climbed up on the carved chest. At the window end of the chest other objects had been piled. The largest of these was something hard and cold to the touch like bronze. The thing had rounded, bell-like sides, and stood almost as high as her waist. It seemed steady enough and if she could climb upon it, she might be able to reach the window.

The sides were slippery and offered no toe hold for her sneakers, but there was a wedge of metal at the top, with a hole through it and she could grasp this and pull herself up. Balancing with one hand against the wall, she managed to reach the window latch. It stuck from long disuse and she struggled with it frantically. Fi-

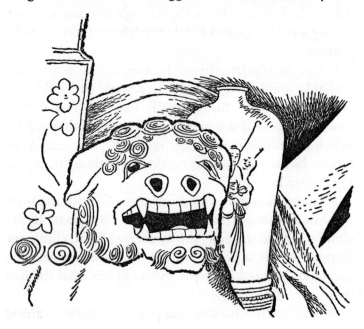

nally it loosened and the little window opened inward. She took several deep breaths of wonderful clean air, feeling like a prisoner just returned to the outer world. In seconds she was perched on the sill, looking downhill over the empty rear garden.

The drop to the ground was more than she wanted to chance, but a tree raised its branches conveniently close. She crawled out on a thick, firm limb, reaching back to pull the window shut. Later she would tell Hana about her adventure and warn her that the window was unlatched. At the moment she was interested only in escape. Crawling along the limb to the trunk, she was able to get down the tree by lowering herself from branch to branch. Near the ground there was a gap where she would have to jump.

She sat astride the lower branch, looking about to make sure no one observed her from the house. Just as she was about to let go and jump, the shrubbery nearby moved and rustled. Someone was there in the garden. Should she climb back up the tree and hide, or jump down and run for freedom before whoever it was stepped out of that shielding clump of bushes?

Before she could decide, the shrubbery waved and rustled again and a man stepped into view. Jill clung to the branch, unable to move. He had evidently seen her, for now he came toward her perch gravely. It was Mr. Tamura and when he reached the tree he made a polite bow.

" Good afternoon," he said.

For a moment Jill was too startled to answer. But he didn't look angry and there was something like a twinkle in the black eyes that were so much like Hana's. Jill put her hands on the branch beneath her and swung herself to the ground.

" The — the window is unlocked," she stated uncomfortably.

" I will fix," said Hana's father. He looked as if he might laugh out loud at any moment and was only restraining himself through politeness. There was no explanation that seemed sensible to give. Jill smiled sheepishly and then ran across the garden, heading for the concealment of the passageway.

Fog drifted in wispy lengths between the walls and

as Jill scooted toward the gate she heard the echo of her own running behind her, as if someone followed. All she wanted now was to escape to the safety of the street. Mr. Tamura would just have to come down and bolt this gate after her.

Not until she was back in the everyday atmosphere of her own street, did she suddenly remember the thing she had climbed upon to get to the window. That cold metal thing with the rounded sides — why, it had been a bell, undoubtedly. Perhaps an old bell from some Oriental temple. Was it, she wondered, the very bell Miss Lydia sometimes thought she heard ringing?

Jill put the thought out of her mind. She didn't want to think about that old house right now. She wanted her mother's company and no queer mysteries, no pop-eyed demons to clutch at her. Potatoes were bubbling in a pan on the stove, and the oven was on, but her mother had taken a break outside while things were cooking. Jill found her on the terrace and saw with surprise what she was doing. Mother, wearing a soft blue sweater, sat on a camp stool out here in the chill mist. A sketching block was propped on her knee and she was drawing. As Jill approached, her mother glanced up at the old house with its turrets tipped by fog.

" Hello, Jill," she said, not looking around. " I'm taking Adrian's remarks to heart, you see. I was a little angry with him at first, but now I've decided to get back to my drawing and really work. No more cunning fashion babies for me."

She had, Jill saw, been sketching the Furness house and she had really caught the eerie spirit of it.

" It's hard to get the impression of mist closing in,"
Mother said. " I'll have to try it again with water col-
ors. The light is fading now. How'm I doing, Jill? "

Jill stepped closer for a better look and almost
gasped. The house rose high above its walls. The top
of a tree was in view and a small window. On the window ledge crouched a figure that looked very much
like Jill.

Jill gulped and looked at her mother. Mother's face
wore an exaggerated innocence that gave her away.

" You — you saw me! " Jill cried.

Mother nodded. " Yes, and I must say I was rather
surprised to see my own child crawl out of a window I
was sketching. Do you think we ought to have a talk
about this, Jill? "

Jill sighed with relief. Now that her secret doings
had been so unexpectedly revealed, all she wanted was
to pour out the story — every bit of it. She had felt
more uncomfortable than she had realized about keeping this from Mother.

" Could I talk to you while you get dinner? " she
asked. " I — I want to tell you all about it right away."

Parents could be the most unexpected people. It
wasn't that Mother approved of what had happened, or
of Jill and Andy going up to the house without Miss
Furness' knowledge. But, nevertheless, Mother was interested in all Jill had to report about Miss Lydia, and
she thought it a shame that anyone so nice should be
kept without friends, though she made the point that
there was probably something more to the behavior of
Matilda Furness than they understood. They ought

not to condemn her without really knowing the reasons behind her actions.

Without knowing how it came about, Jill found herself telling everybody about her afternoon adventure right at the dinner table that night. Mr. Dallas laughed out loud over the episode of the window.

" Wish I could have seen that, Jill," he said.

Mother tried to look shocked. " For goodness' sakes, don't encourage her, Roger. After all, Miss Furness is in charge of her house and there mustn't be any more visits without her knowledge."

Jill had to grin at the wink of sympathy Mr. Dallas gave her, but she felt crestfallen at the thought of no more visits.

" Golly! " Andy wailed. " To think I had to miss the last trip! "

Adrian forgot to be sniffy and asked questions about the roomful of objects from the Orient. At least this was one dinner when they were not separated into opposing teams. They were almost like one family and Jill sensed that Mr. Dallas was somehow pleased by what had happened.

By the time dishes were done, they were still talking. Adrian had just suggested that Jill might find some of those old books by Lydia von Wallenstein in the public library, when the door chimes rang. Andy went to answer and a moment later he was back, wearing a somewhat stunned look as he invited Miss Matilda Furness into the living room.

11

COIT TOWER

Miss Matilda wore her black hat with the rusty-black rosettes and she looked extremely commanding as she sat facing the others. Mother managed to seem the least astonished person in the group and she welcomed their guest as if Matilda Furness made a habit of dropping in on them. Mr. Dallas was both interested and faintly amused.

As she curled up on an ottoman near her mother, Jill was thankful that all secrets were out and that both Mother and Mr. Dallas knew everything ahead of time.

To Jill's surprise, however, Miss Furness seemed little concerned with Jill's visit to her sister that afternoon. She addressed herself directly to Mr. Dallas.

"My sister has told me," she said grimly, "that you are the Roger Dallas who writes for the newspapers. Is she correct about this?"

Mr. Dallas admitted his identity.

"Lydia also tells me that you are interested in our house and family and have been harboring the intention of writing about us in your paper."

This time Mr. Dallas looked surprised and Jill felt her ears getting hot, for she had rather elaborated on what had been only a casual remark made by Mr. Dallas.

" I am certainly interested in San Francisco history," he said calmly. " I may even have expressed some curiosity about your house. Most old houses have stories behind them. But I have no intention of disturbing your privacy, or prying where my interest isn't welcome."

Miss Matilda clasped black-gloved hands in her lap. She looked, Jill thought, a little like that figure of Buddha in the curio room.

" I am relieved indeed to hear that," Miss Furness said. " After my sister's report this afternoon, I was afraid we might be submitted to some further unpleasantness from the press."

She glanced sharply from Mr. Dallas to Mother and back again. In the second when her eyes were not upon him, Mr. Dallas gave Jill another conspirator's wink. That surely meant that he wasn't cross because she had repeated his remark.

The black rosettes on Miss Furness' hat nodded regally as she continued. " My sister Lydia was in Yokohama at the time of the great Japanese earthquake of '23. The house she was in was partially demolished and she was severely injured. This frightful catastrophe occurred some months after her husband was lost in the interior of China. When she was brought home to me, half paralyzed, an invalid, she was a pitiful and tragic figure. Because of both her husband's fame and her own distinction as an author, we were persistently annoyed by reporters. There was a great deal of unpleasantness — injurious to my sister's health. I had to shut my door upon the press and refuse to let anyone come near her."

For the first time Miss Furness seemed less frightening. Even as she sat there, ramrod stiff, her mouth straight and unsmiling, she seemed to have changed subtly. She wasn't stern and cruel as she had appeared, but only a woman who was truly concerned about a sister she loved.

" I can see that it has been necessary to protect your sister," Mr. Dallas said courteously.

" Exactly," said Miss Furness, with an air of having finished her business.

Before their visitor could rise from her chair, Mother spoke in a little rush.

" From what Jill has told me, your sister has enjoyed having two young visitors. Do you really feel that she should not have this small pleasure? "

Miss Furness stiffened. " I am the best judge of that. My sister has forgotten many of the tragic things that have happened to her. As long as she doesn't recall them she can be happy in the present. Outsiders disturb her, say the wrong things, stir her memory. Then she begins to confuse the past with the present. She rambles about — all sorts of things."

" Like the green cat? " said Jill, surprising herself as much as anyone else.

" What do you know about a green cat? " Miss Matilda asked sharply.

" Only — only that she keeps wishing she could find it," Jill said. She threw Andy a look that pleaded for help.

" It seemed to be awfully important to her," said Andy.

The carved, stern face of Matilda Furness seemed to crumple a little and she appeared suddenly less sure of herself. " I have no idea what she means by that reference to a green cat. She used to ask for it again and again when she first came home and was ill and in delirium. I presume it was something she must have treasured in the Orient, something that was lost in the quake. But when I've tried to get her to explain she becomes terribly upset. There seems to be a conflict in her between wanting the thing, whatever it is, and yet being afraid to find it again. In any case, I hope you understand why she must not be disturbed by strangers, however friendly they may be."

Miss Furness had said her final say. She rose and sailed toward the door with that air of leading an army which Jill had noted before.

" You know," Roger Dallas said when Miss Furness had gone, " I can't help feeling that there's something more to Miss Lydia's story than meets the eye. Something more, I mean, than losing her husband or being in a terrible earthquake. Disasters happen to people and they recover and get over them. This smacks of unfinished business to me. There's something back there that's tormenting Miss Lydia. I'm sure of it."

" That's what I think! " Jill cried. " If we could just find that green cat — "

Adrian, staring at his feet, had taken no part in the discussion, but now he spoke directly to Jill.

" If you're any kind of a detective," he said, " I

should think you'd go to the library, or down to Dad's office and look up old newspapers around the time when Lydia von Wallenstein arrived in San Francisco. Probably that was a little while after that big earthquake in Japan. Miss Furness said she had to shut out the reporters because of their unpleasant curiosity. Perhaps the reporters themselves tell something about that."

This seemed a good idea, even if it did come from Adrian.

"That reminds me!" Mother cried, though it wasn't at all apparent what had reminded her of what. She dashed into the kitchen and came back with the sketch she had drawn of the Furness house.

"What do you think of this as a beginning?" she asked, holding the sketch out to Adrian.

Carol, who was not being consulted, came over right away to look at the picture. "That's the Furness house!" she announced with an air of discovery.

Mother smiled. "At least that means nobody will take it for the Coit Tower." But she was still waiting for Adrian, who soberly studied the picture.

Jill watched him, feeling that it was pretty risky of her mother to ask Adrian's opinion about anything.

When he handed the sketch block back to Mother he gave her his rare, flashing smile. "That's awfully good. You ought to go ahead and finish it. Though I'm not sure that queer thing stuck in the window really belongs in the picture."

Mother thanked Adrian hastily and said she'd be grateful for any criticism he might give her. Jill thought it was silly for Mother, who was a professional artist and had earned her living by her drawing, to ask a kid like Adrian for his opinion. Consulting him like that would make him more conceited than ever. But at least peace reigned in the Dallas household for that evening and everyone seemed more comfortable, now that Adrian wasn't sulking.

Mr. Dallas smiled over the picture and looked pleased with Adrian. It was plain that he wanted very much to have Adrian be nice to Emily.

Adrian's change of disposition held through to Sunday, and in spite of her earlier annoyance with him Jill found herself ready to be friends with him again. There was no one more charming and winning than Adrian when he wanted to be.

They planned to leave for the Coit Tower around 11:30 Sunday morning. They would take a lunch box and spend some time on Telegraph Hill. Mother told Jill privately that she would be glad to have them out of the house because she was going to practice her shish kebab recipe today. She couldn't risk a surprise dish that might turn out wrong.

At the last minute one of Carol's friends invited her to an outing in Golden Gate Park and Mother decided to let her go there instead. It would be more fun for Carol to be with someone her own age.

Hana appeared right on time and Mr. Dallas drove the four over to the Coit Tower; they were to come home by bus. On the way Hana and Jill listened with interest while Adrian, who could when he felt like it talk more easily and fluently than Andy, told them about the tall white tower that rose from its nest of greenery on Telegraph Hill.

In the long-ago days when San Francisco was young there had been a semaphore up there that signaled to ships at sea. That was how the hill got its name. Later, during the lifetime of Lillie Hitchcock Coit there was no signal tower on the hill. Lillie was one of the most colorful figures in San Francisco's colorful past. As a girl she rode with the engines of her favorite fire company to every fire they attended. In fact she was made an honorary fireman in the company and continued to ride to fires long after she was a married woman.

When she died some years earlier, Adrian went on, she left a sum of money for the city to build a memorial which would help to beautify San Francisco. There had been quite a few arguments when the tower was built because there were some who called it a smoke stack and other unflattering names, and said it did not beautify anything. But it was a wonderful way to get a view of the whole San Francisco area, and by now it had become such a familiar landmark that people were developing an affection for it.

Mr. Dallas drove up the last stretch of the winding road that led to the crown of Telegraph Hill and let the children off. It was a bright and lovely day, but as usual a strong wind blew in from the sea and Jill was glad that she and Hana had brought sweaters along. At the base of the tower was a circular clearing where cars could park. Licenses from all over the country revealed how interested tourists were in this spot.

Hana had not been up here before and she and Jill

could hardly decide which way to look first — up at the dizzy structure of the tower, or out over the parapet at the many views of the city.

Andy had brought his camera and he posed the other three against the background of the tower. He had just snapped a picture, when a car drew up nearby and a man and a woman got out. Jill noted idly that the license was from Ohio. The woman, who was rather plump and wore a hat difficult to handle in this wind, started toward them, leaving her husband to study the car's tires. She saw Adrian posing between the two girls and gave a squeal of delighted discovery.

" Adrian Dallas! " she cried, sailing toward them, clinging to her hat. " And Andy too — how wonderful to see you both again! Goodness, how you've grown in the last four years! Why, the last time I saw you you were only so high."

Jill and Hana exchanged looks as they watched. It was funny how grownups always went through that my-how-you-have-grown routine. What did they expect you to do — stand still? Andy slung his camera over his shoulder and grinned at the woman.

" Hello, Mrs. Brewster. I didn't know you were back in San Francisco."

" We're on vacation," the woman said and turned to beckon commandingly to her husband. " Henry — do stop worrying about those old tires and come see who's here. Adrian and Andy Dallas! "

Mrs. Brewster had a well-fed look, but her husband was thin as a string bean and quiet as a clam. He smiled and came over to shake hands with the boys, but he

left most of the talking to his wife. She hardly listened
while Adrian introduced Jill and Hana, though she
nodded vaguely in the girls' direction. Her attention
was upon this reunion with the sons of an old friend.

" How is your mother, boys? I've been out of touch
with San Francisco for so long. She is one of the people
I want to call and have a good visit with. Do tell me,
Adrian — "

She broke off because of the way in which Adrian was
staring at her, while Andy examined his knuckles and
turned red to the ears. Mr. Brewster looked from one
boy to the other and nudged his wife, but she went
right on.

" Gracious! What's wrong? Your mother isn't ill, is
she? "

Adrian regarded her coldly. " Mother died two years
ago," he said.

Mrs. Brewster looked like a fish out of water, gasp-
ing for air. It was her husband who spoke kindly to the
boys.

" We're sorry," he said gently. " Terribly sorry. We
didn't know."

" Your father should have written us! " Mrs. Brewster had recovered the power of speech. " This is really a terrible shock. I can hardly believe that dear
Margaret is gone. And your poor father — how lonely
he must be. Oh, we must drop in to see him while we're
here. Do you suppose tomorrow night — "

Adrian's lips were straight and thin. " My father,"
he said clearly, " has married again. And I don't think

he will be home tomorrow night." He glanced at his companions who were watching him uncomfortably. " If we're going up the tower, come along," he told them.

He didn't wait to see if they would follow, but stalked toward the steps that led to the tower's base. Andy mumbled a good-by to the Brewsters and went after his brother. As Jill and Hana followed, Jill saw Mr. Brewster put a hand on his wife's arm.

Adrian paid for their tickets to the tower elevator and they got into the car in silence. Other visitors joined them and they rode to the top without saying a word. Jill felt awfully sorry for Adrian, who was taking this so hard, but she had no idea what to say to him, or how to help him. She and Hana went to a tower window together to look out over the city. Andy stood beside his brother at another window and Jill heard them speaking in low tones.

The view up here was tremendous. They were looking toward Russian Hill and the streets of San Francisco went straight away beneath the tower and straight up the opposite hills, as if somebody had ruled lines on a piece of paper, paying no attention to the heights.

Hana, who had been quiet during Mrs. Brewster's outburst, pointed across the city calmly. Her own good manners kept her from showing that she realized anything unfortunate had happened.

" You see little street with white houses and many flowers over there? This is crookedest street in whole world. Name is Lombard Avenue."

On one steep patch near the top of a hill, the usual straight line had been turned into zigzag curves of pavement, winding back and forth between bright flower beds that glowed with color even at this distance.

When they had looked long enough, the girls moved around to another vantage point and a new view. Looking down upon the town like this they could see unexpected patches of garden here and there, hidden from the streets, but apparently shared by houses around them. Many of the Telegraph Hill roof tops held clotheslines and even on Sunday there were lines of washing flapping in the wind.

As the girls edged around the tower, they came next to Andy and Adrian. Adrian stared gloomily toward the Berkeley shore across the Bay and did not even glance at Jill and Hana. It was Andy who pointed out various sights, while Adrian, lost in his own unhappy thoughts, paid no attention.

" After the big earthquake that started the fire in 1906," Andy said, " just about everything in sight was burned. I've seen pictures of it. In three days' time all this was four square miles of rubble. Just a few houses stood on Russian Hill — like the Furness house, and some of the Italian homes here on Telegraph Hill. Nob Hill was practically wiped out, though the outside part of the Flood mansion stood and it was built up again."

When the girls had seen enough they all returned to the elevator, ready now to find a spot where they could eat lunch and then explore Telegraph Hill. Andy said he knew a woodsy pathway and a place where they could spread out their things and be comfortable on the leeward side of the hill. There the sun shone warmly and the wind didn't blow so hard. But Adrian held back.

" You go ahead if you want to," he said. I'm going home."

12

JILL SPEAKS HER MIND

JILL felt all her recent impatience with Adrian surge up more strongly than ever. He couldn't go home! She could imagine just what might happen if he showed up suddenly at home right when Mother was serving a shish kebab dish that had probably gone wrong. Especially in his present mood.

" Why are you going home? " she asked straight out.

His gray eyes flicked her with a look of dislike. " If you want to know," he said, " I'm bored."

Hana acted quickly. This was evidently a family fight and she must have known the best thing to do, the most courteous thing, was to take herself out of ear- shot. She limped over to a cement step and became very busy taking off a shoe to look inside for an imaginary stone.

" Oh, look now," Andy said to his brother, " don't let somebody like Mrs. Brewster spoil your day."

" Nobody's spoiling my day," Adrian snapped. " I'm going home — that's all."

He had been carrying the lunch box and now he handed it abruptly to Andy. But, before he could stalk off down the hill, Jill lost her last trace of patience and her temper as well.

"You listen here, Adrian Dallas!" she burst out. "You're a year older than I am, but sometimes you act as if you were younger than Carol. I don't see why we should baby you all the time. Everybody thinks you're so sensitive and that we must be careful of your feelings. But you're only sensitive about *you*. You don't care anything at all about how much you hurt other people's feelings. You don't care how mean you are to my mother and even to your own brother. Why don't you grow up?"

Adrian stared at her in astonishment. Plainly he was not used to being talked to in such a manner. But before he could recover, Jill got her breath and went back into battle.

"You could learn a lot about manners from Hana Tamura. She's our guest today, and how do you think she feels at being told that you're bored with her? What about her feelings? They're just as important as yours! And besides, I remember something my father used to tell us. Mother says he always claimed that smart people never get bored — only stupid ones. He said smart people can always find something to interest them anywhere they are. So maybe you're not as smart as you think you are, Mister Adrian Dallas!"

By that time Jill was so mad she was shaking. Her words were tumbling over one another and the look of shock in Adrian's face had begun to scare her. So she did exactly the thing she always hated most to do when she got mad — she burst into tears.

" Oh, gosh! " Andy said. " Don't cry, Jill. Adrian's not as bad as you think."

Jill searched her pocket for a handkerchief and blew her nose loudly. She didn't dare look at Adrian. Now she had done it. Now he'd never come with them for lunch and everything would be spoiled, both here and at home.

Adrian surprised her. " I guess maybe I am," he said quietly to his brother. " I mean I am as bad as she thinks."

Jill blinked at him through her tears and saw that the Adrian who was watching her in this new, worried way had all his defenses down. He looked like a person who had stood up to a slapping that had left him a little dizzy.

" I don't agree with everything you've said," he told her. " But I guess I had some of it coming. O.K., I'll stay with the party." He gave her a shaky sort of smile. " And I dare you to bore me! "

He walked over to Hana, who was now earnestly searching her other shoe. Jill glanced at Andy. There were beads of perspiration across his forehead and she felt sorrier for him than she did for Adrian. Andy, she suspected, was the one who felt things a lot more deeply than his brother did. But he felt them about other people, as well as about himself. She was lucky to have a brother like Andy.

" I'm sorry," she told him humbly. " I'm the one who needs to grow up and not go getting mad like that."

" It's O.K.," Andy said, never at ease with words.

" Adrian didn't really want to go off and leave us. I expect he's glad something happened so he could stay."

How well Andy knew his brother! Jill thought, beginning to feel better herself. Adrian came back with Hana beside him, and now he was all cheerfulness again.

" I'm hungry," he said — as if everything were just the way it had been before Mrs. Brewster had left her car. " Let's find that place to eat."

As they followed a path that led beneath evergreens and eucalyptus trees, Jill couldn't help but wonder if her words had really had any effect on Adrian at all. Perhaps they had only shamed him, so that he felt it necessary to reinstate himself in their eyes. She couldn't return so quickly to an easy, natural manner after her own outburst. When they found a place where they could sit down and open their sandwiches, she was glad that Hana took the boys' attention with an invitation she had apparently been saving.

" My mother will like if you come to have Japanese dinner end of this week. She will make *sukiyaki* just like in Japan if you will prease to come."

" At the Furness house? " Andy asked in astonishment. And added quickly: " Why, sure. That sounds like fun."

" My father talks to Miss Furness and she is saying O.K. But we must not to disturb Miss Rydia."

Even Adrian liked the idea and put himself out to be gracious about the invitation. Nevertheless, Jill continued to watch him warily.

When they'd eaten everything down to the last

crumb they packed the wrappings and peelings away
in the lunch box so the next fellow who came along
would never know anyone had picnicked here. Then
they trailed after Andy as he led them across side
streets, up and down steps, and along narrow wooden
walks that seemed suspended among the bright gardens that crowded this side of Telegraph Hill. Never
had Jill seen so many geraniums. They grew profusely
everywhere — in boxes, through fences, down banks.

It was warm and sunny here and agreeably still,
though the trees higher up shook and rustled in the
wind. The little houses clung to steep cliffs, their gardens gay with birds and flowers. It was like another
world — a suspended, arboreal sort of world.

It was so much fun to take odd turns and climb up
and down unexpected flights of steps that they hardly
noticed when the sun vanished in the usual afternoon
mist, rolling in through the Golden Gate. Andy was
the first to look up and hold out his hand in astonishment.

" Why, it's raining," he said, with the air of one unable to believe his own eyes.

They scurried for shelter under the trees and waited
for the shower to pass. According to Andy it had no
business raining at this time of the year. Rain was a
serious business in San Francisco and it was supposed
to arrive later on, not now.

When the afternoon ended and they took a bus
home, everyone seemed to be on friendly and comfortable terms. Jill had a chance for a good visit with Hana,
while the boys sat up ahead. Hana explained that her

father had been in this country for many years, working for Miss Furness. A few years before the war with Japan he had gone home for a visit and had married Hana's mother. Mrs. Tamura had been timid about coming to this country and her husband had returned alone, hoping to bring her here later.

" I am born in Japan and am very small when the war comes," said Hana, shaking her head sadly. " My father must stay here and American Government does not permit us to come to San Francisco until last year."

The two girls were silent for a little while, and Jill thought about Hana growing up without knowing her father until recently. Then she asked how Hana liked the United States.

The other girl's face brightened and she admitted that she liked it very much, though sometimes at first she was homesick for her friends in Japan. She did not have many friends in San Francisco as yet, though she had found one whom she especially liked — a Chinese girl who lived in Chinatown. Today had been wonderful, Hana said, and expressed her gratitude and enjoyment several times.

Jill felt that in spite of Adrian's sulks and her own outburst, the day had really been a success. Now she could look forward with pleasure to the invitation to a Japanese dinner with the Tamuras later in the week.

When they reached home Mother whispered to Jill that the special dish had not turned out very well, but she knew what her mistake had been and was ready to try again. Jill felt doubly thankful that Adrian had not left them and come home.

On Monday Andy offered to go to the public library with Jill and help her look up old papers which might carry the story of the return of Mrs. Karl von Wallenstein to San Francisco sometimes during the year 1923. She was glad to have his help in the search.

This was the first time Jill had seen San Francisco's Civic Center, where beautiful buildings clustered together in a group. The public library was one of these, facing the impressive domed City Hall. They went inside the handsome entryway to find a wide marble staircase leading to the second floor. The newspaper room was at the end of a main floor corridor and Andy knew his way to it. When he had explained what they wanted, the two were permitted inside where they could spread out a huge bound volume of newspapers for the year of the Japanese earthquake.

Some of the pictures and news headings of the time looked interesting and sometimes Jill was tempted to stop and read. The Sunday magazine sections of this particular paper were arresting and startling. They seemed to be made up of lurid stories of mysteries and murders and scandals, illustrated with fearful and exaggerated drawings.

" We'll never find anything if you stop to read that junk," Andy protested. So Jill let him turn the magazine section over quickly and get to the news.

While Andy ran down the page on one side, checking every item, Jill took the other. There was considerable news about the earthquake in Japan, but not until that had died out did Jill's searching finger come upon the name of Karl von Wallenstein. She and Andy read the piece together eagerly.

The account mentioned that nothing had been heard from the explorer in many months. The last word of the expedition had come with the finding of the body of von Wallenstein's partner — an American named Frederick Parke. Parke had been shot under mysterious circumstances, but there was no trace of the rest of the party. Some of the native bearers had deserted earlier when the expedition went into bandit territory, and it was presumed that von Wallenstein had been taken by bandits.

Then, for the first time, came mention of his wife. Baroness Lydia von Wallenstein, an American, and a member of an old San Francisco family, had been severely injured in the earthquake which had destroyed her home in Yokohama. She was now on board a ship coming to America.

More searching through news in the following days brought mention of Lydia's arrival in San Francisco. The report said she was taken to her sister's home on Russian Hill, where Miss Furness was nursing her. There followed in the next few days several interviews with Miss Furness. Lydia, it seemed, was too ill to be interviewed. Everything seemed to be on amiable enough terms between Matilda and the reporters, however. Then, after an interval of some days came a brief notice to the effect that Miss Furness had closed her door upon all reporters and would see no one from a newspaper or magazine. The reporter seemed a bit indignant about this. But that, unless Jill and Andy had missed something, was the end of the news. No further searching revealed anything.

Andy closed the big volume and he and Jill looked at each other in bafflement.

" What do you think happened? " Jill asked.

Andy shook his head. " I suppose Miss Furness got tired of reporters."

Jill remained doubtful. It seemed odd that Matilda Furness had been friendly enough at first and had then suddenly shut her door in every face, closed herself and her sister away from all outsiders. The few bits of information printed contained nothing that might upset anyone so severely, but Miss Furness herself had said there had been unpleasantness.

There was no use trying to guess what might have happened. In one respect Jill was especially disappointed. She had hoped that somewhere along the line there might be a reference to Miss Lydia's green cat. But the cat, whatever and wherever it was, had not been important enough to rate newspaper mention.

There was, however, one report that had mentioned a bronze temple bell. It had been a Japanese bell and not one sent back from an expedition of the baron's. Apparently it was one of the few things in Lydia's Japanese house that had not been destroyed in the disaster, and it had been brought home on the same boat with its owner.

" I wonder why she thinks she hears that bell ringing? " Jill pondered to Andy. " And I wonder if that's the bell I climbed on in the curio room."

Andy had no answer and she could only hope that something unexpected might happen on the night they had dinner with the Tamuras, something that would, after all, enable them to see Miss Lydia again.

As a matter of fact, on the night they went to dinner, something of the sort happened almost at once. When Adrian, Andy, Jill, and Carol went up the steps to ring the front doorbell of the Furness house, Hana came smiling to let them into the big hall. There were more lights tonight, in honor of company, and as they followed Hana through the house, walking quietly because of the hush that always lay over the place, Jill glanced up to see Miss Matilda Furness watching them from the shadowy balcony above.

" Good evening, children." She wasn't exactly smiling, but she wasn't scowling at them either. " When you've finished dinner," she went on, " I wonder if you would stop in very briefly to speak to my sister? "

Andy showed no surprise. " Sure," he said, " we'd like to." But Jill stared in such astonishment that Miss Furness seemed uncomfortable under her look.

" I must admit," she said tartly, " that my sister seems to have been considerably cheered by her visits with you young people. I don't think you should stay more than a few minutes tonight, but perhaps such a visit will do her no harm."

Jill and Andy exchanged looks as they followed Hana to the back of the house. " That's a score for our side," said Andy under his breath. It was a good thing, Jill thought, that Miss Furness did not know about the escapade of one of her visitors in the curio room.

13

THE TEMPLE BELL

Hana and her parents had comfortable quarters on a level even with the hill at the back of the house. Jill found, to her interest, that one room had been completely done over in the Japanese manner.

Hana smiled at her surprise. " Miss Furness makes special place for my mother when she comes. Just like in Japan. Here we can sleep on good hard beds we roll out on floor. Must take off shoes now."

A fine yellowish colored matting covered the floor of this one room and of course they could not step onto it with American shoes. Mrs. Tamura, who was not much taller than Hana, met them graciously at the door and invited them in. She looked charming in a pink-and-gray flowered kimono.

The room was without furnishings except for several small black-lacquer tables only a few inches high, set in a row in the middle of the *tatami* matting. Opposite each table was a thin cushion of black satin, embroidered in gold, and Hana indicated that they were to sit on these. The walls had been papered in a plain light buff, though Hana explained that this was not like Japan. A real Japanese house would have sliding screens with rice paper panes for the walls of the room.

When Mr. Tamura came to greet them, it seemed to Jill that he still had a quirk to his smile as he bowed to her. She remembered all too well her last undignified meeting with him.

The grownups did not sit with them at the little tables, since this was a party for the young people. Mr.

Tamura withdrew and Hana helped her pretty little mother.

Andy and Adrian had often eaten in Chinatown, so they could handle chopsticks with some skill, though the Japanese kind, they said, were shorter than the Chinese. Carol and Jill had never held a pair in their hands before and they had trouble in spite of Hana's patient teaching.

The meal itself was not only delicious, but every dish was as beautiful as a picture in its careful arrangement. Adrian's artistic eye noted everything and tonight he seemed to be in a cheerful mood.

There was a clear soup, with tiny flowerlike snips of vegetable floating in it. This was served in covered bowls. Then came *tempura*, which was large shrimp fried in batter. This was dipped into a brown salty sauce. Carol speared hers ungracefully with one chopstick, but Jill imitated Hana and picked up the shrimp in her fingers by the hard-shell tail.

The main dish was cooked over an electric burner right before them. Small pieces of beef had been cut paper thin and arranged with a variety of vegetables on a huge platter. From this servings were slid into the heated pan, to give off an odor that made everyone hungrier than ever as the mixture cooked.

Hana was very gay and happy tonight, darting about like a small humming bird, playing hostess and helping her mother. Once Adrian, who had been eating his mixture of rice and beef in thoughtful silence, startled Jill with a sudden remark.

" Do you suppose," he said to no one in particular.

" that Miss Furness might let me see the curio room if I asked her? "

Mrs. Tamura did not speak much English and she did not understand, but Hana looked at him doubtfully. She seemed to be a little afraid of Adrian since Sunday and not anxious to commit herself.

Jill said at once that she thought it was a good idea to try. " After all, Miss Furness can't do more than say no. And she might let you in." Adrian, as Jill had to admit, at times had a more grown-up manner than the rest of them, and he could be very charming when he chose.

Adrian had his chance more quickly than he expected because Miss Furness herself came to the door of the room while they were still eating. Hana offered her a bowl of *sukiyaki,* but she shook her head. Her sister would probably enjoy some, but she preferred plain American cooking.

Adrian got up from his cushion and spoke to Miss Furness without the slightest hesitation.

" I don't know whether Jill has mentioned it or not," he said, " but I'm studying art and I'm especially interested just now in objects from the Orient. Jill says you have a roomful of things up here and I wondered — "

Miss Furness fixed Jill with a quick, sharp look and spoke before he had time to finish. " Ah, yes. I believe this young lady has already made the acquaintance of that room. You were in it the other day, weren't you? "

Jill nearly choked on a tender piece of bamboo shoot. So Miss Furness knew? Had she known all along and locked her in on purpose?

" I — I got mixed up and went to the wrong door,"
Jill said sheepishly. " I didn't mean to go in there."

" Then you might at least have let me know you were
there when I locked the door," said Miss Furness.

" I was afraid to," Jill said, staring at the tips of Miss
Furness' black shoes, unable to raise her eyes to the
stern face above.

" I recall climbing out that window myself as a
child," Miss Furness said. " That tree was younger
then, but it reached to the window. Though I must say
I was surprised when I looked out from the floor above
and saw what you were doing."

Jill could feel her whole face grow warm. She had
thought at the time no one had seen her — but it
seemed that practically the whole hillside had been
watching. Mr. Tamura, Mother, and now Miss Furness. She had no words left at all.

Miss Furness returned her attention to Adrian.
" After you've said good evening to my sister, I'll open
the room for you. Since you are interested, I see no
reason why you shouldn't have a look at the collection.
But please don't mention these things to my sister.
They carry too many unhappy memories. I've told her
I use the room for storage and I try to keep it locked. I
shall, of course, trust you to see that nothing is dam-
aged."

Adrian assured her courteously that he would take
care of that and, when he sat down at the little table
again, he gave Jill an odd look. Perhaps, she thought
uncomfortably, he was remembering the way she had
kicked over his vase of brushes and broken it. She must

be very, very careful. She couldn't imagine anything more awful than to bring Miss Furness' wrath upon herself by damaging something valuable in that room. At least she was glad Adrian had made his daring request. There was something in the curio room she wanted to have another look at. Perhaps she would now have a chance.

For dessert there was American chocolate ice cream, accompanied by little rice cakes folded and puffed so that they resembled little envelopes.

" Cakes are Chinese, not Japanese," Hana explained. " My friend Lotus Wang in Chinatown make me present of this cakes."

" You'll find your fortunes inside," said Andy, breaking his cake to show them the tiny strip of paper hidden beneath the hard crust. He read it aloud, laughing. " ' Fame will come if you persevere.' I'm afraid the fortune gods have got me mixed up with Adrian. I'm not the one who'll be famous. What does yours say, Adrian? "

Adrian crumbled the brown crust in his fingers and took out the slip. " ' Many friends will be your lot if you continue to smile,' " he read, grinning wryly.

That was hitting home, thought Jill. She was saving her own cake till the others had been read.

Carol's said simply, " ' Your heart's wish is on the way,' " and she laughed. " That means I'll get to do a solo in the fall entertainment, even if I am new in town."

Hana read hers: " ' A tall man will come into your life, bringing good fortune.' " That was funny because almost anyone would look tall to Hana.

It was Jill's turn and she broke her cake and nibbled at the crisp pieces while she picked up the fortune slip. But the words this time were so odd that she was startled. She read them aloud in a surprised tone.

" ' Be careful when you tread among cats, as claws may scratch.' "

Nobody could make much sense of that, but Jill, even though she didn't believe in fortune-telling, wondered if this had anything to do with a green cat.

When the meal was over, Hana went with them to Miss Lydia's rooms and knocked on the door. Miss Furness was there and she stayed watchfully with the young people while they visited her sister.

Miss Lydia was delighted to see them. " I've been waiting to meet the dancing sister and the painting brother," she said.

The big bare room, with all its furniture pushed back against the walls to allow for easy passage of Miss Lydia's wheel chair, appealed to Carol. In fact, it took no coaxing at all for Miss Lydia to persuade her to dance for them. Jill sighed and sat down with the others to watch. Once Carol had the spotlight, there was no telling how long something like this might go on. Fortunately — from Jill's viewpoint — Carol didn't have her ballet slippers, the radio music wasn't right, and a commercial interrupted Carol's performance. But Miss Lydia seemed to enjoy the sampling and led the applause.

Miss Furness permitted them to remain with her sister only a little while. Then she remembered her promise about the curio room and took them back to it. She unlocked the double doors, turned on some lights, and the whole weird collection sprang into dusty life.

Carol squealed and shivered, but would not return to the hall. " It's fun to be scared," she admitted.

Adrian moved delightedly among gods and animals carved chests and stone lanterns. Carefully, Jill led Andy to the place where books were stacked on the floor, but she kept her eye mainly on the temple bell. She had a notion about that bell, but she didn't want to attract Miss Furness' attention to her curiosity. She was very careful, even in picking up a book, lest something calamitous happen that would cause a collapse or a landslide among these treasures.

Andy turned a few pages of the book and then spoke to Miss Furness across the room. " This was written by your sister, wasn't it? Would you let us read one of these books? This one on India sounds interesting."

Miss Furness did not easily say yes to anything. She had been accustomed to saying no for too long a time. But, after due thought, she seemed to find no reason for refusing.

" You may borrow one of them, if you like," she said. " But please wash your hands before reading it and don't tear the pages."

Jill and Andy glanced at each other. She must think them about three years old.

Miss Furness' attention wandered about the room and she shook her head sadly. " I know we shouldn't keep all these things. They belong in a museum and goodness knows almost any museum would be happy to

have them. But they really belong to my sister and I
feel I have no right to dispose of them without her con-
sent. Yet I don't want her to be upset with old memories as she would certainly be if she came in here. It's
better to keep them locked up for the present and let
the museums wait."

Jill sensed that she was merely thinking out loud and
expected no answer. Just then Hana, who had stayed
behind with Miss Lydia, came to call Matilda to her
sister. Miss Furness gave a quick look around the
room, said, " Be very careful, children. I'll be right
back," and disappeared through the doorway.

Jill flew into action. " The bell! " she whispered to
Andy. " It's right over there. Miss Lydia keeps thinking
she hears a bell ringing. Do you think that one could
be rung? "

Andy came over to look at the bronze bell. " I don't
see how it could be rung unless it was suspended from
something," he said. " Adrian, you know about stuff
like this — how would a temple bell be rung? "

" Maybe with a mallet, or some sort of padded stick,"
Adrian said. " I don't know whether this type of bell
has a clapper inside. Anyway what difference does it
make? "

" Not any difference, as far as I can see," Andy admitted, " since Miss Lydia only hears it in her imagination. What's your notion, Jill? "

" I just wondered what would happen if she heard
the real bell ringing," Jill said.

The musty old room was shut away from sun and
heat and it began to seem cold in here. She drew her

hand away from the chill surface of the bell.

" Let's tip it over and see if there's a clapper inside," Adrian suggested to Andy. " I'd be interested to know how it was rung."

Both boys took hold of the metal wedge at the top of the bell and slowly began to tip the whole thing over. Carol squealed and covered her ears, and even Jill expected to hear a crash. She hoped they wouldn't end up by dropping it and breaking something.

But the bell, being hollow, wasn't terribly heavy, and the boys tipped it on its side on top of the chest. The hollow interior was stuffed with newspapers and what looked like wads of old blanket. It must have been packed like that for shipping, and the stuffing materials had never been removed. Forgetting her caution, Jill helped Adrian and Andy pull out the crumbly wads of paper and scraps of stuffing.

Adrian held up a piece of newspaper curiously. It was printed in Oriental characters that ran in vertical lines up and down the page. However, the next bit Jill pulled out bore English lettering. It was a page from *The Yokohama Gazette* dated before the great earthquake. This bell had apparently not been unpacked in all the years it had stood here in this dark room. Perhaps Miss Furness had just ordered it put in here with the other things and had never looked at it again.

Andy reached in to pull out more stuffing — they were getting to the inside of the bell now, where the clapper would be, if there was one. As he pulled, Jill saw a lumpy something come loose and slide to the lip of the bell. She caught it just in time and held up the package. An object of some sort had been wrapped and rewrapped in folds of torn blanket.

" There's something here," Jill said. " Let's see what it is."

" Probably the clapper, or tongue, or whatever you call it," said Adrian, but she didn't think he was right. This didn't feel like that, and anyway why should an old metal clapper be wrapped up so carefully?

Prickling excitement ran through Jill as her hands felt beneath the wrappings to find a cool china surface, an irregular surface that had been shaped into a certain mold — an almost familiar mold.

She let the last scrap of blanket fall to the floor and held the object up to the light. Andy stared in fascination and Adrian gave a low whistle.

The thing in Jill's hands was a pale-green, glazed china figure, the figure of a creature that resembled a cat. The animal sat tall and elongated, nearly a foot high. Its green tail was curled about its toes and its body was very catlike. The eyes were shaped like a cat's and so were the pricked-up ears, one of which had been chipped. But the mouth was something else. The lips drew thinly back in a snarl, showing a double row of fearsome teeth and a thick tongue. Whoever had made this creature had chosen to give it the mouth of an angry dragon. The eyes too were odd, in that they were only sockets. Black slits shaped like the eyes of a cat had been cut through the clay surface to the hollow interior.

With its blank eyes the creature looked at the four children, mysteriously wise, mysteriously alive, as if it knew the secrets of the years.

No one was aware that Miss Furness had returned until they heard her speak sharply from the doorway.

" What have you there? Where did you find that green cat? "

14

IN THE NIGHT

Adrian recovered first and answered Miss Furness. "This was wrapped up carefully and stuffed into the bell," he said. "It looks like something from China."

Miss Furness came slowly toward him around the intervening objects in the room. Adrian held out the pale-green cat, but she drew back almost as if she were afraid to touch it.

"This must be the one," Jill said, hardly aware that she spoke. "This must be the green cat that Miss Lydia is always asking for."

"Maybe we ought to take it to her," Andy said.

Miss Furness spoke quickly. "No! I don't want her upset. I don't want her to remember. Not one of you is to mention it to her ever. Do you understand?"

Andy agreed and Jill was forced to nod unwillingly. Only Adrian, who was turning the odd figure about in his hands, paid no attention. Adrian had little interest in whether or not Miss Lydia saw the cat. He didn't even know about her asking for a green cat. There was only one thought in Adrian's mind.

" It's a very interesting piece," he said. " The workmanship is rather crude, but awfully effective. This may be old and valuable, Miss Furness. Would you let me borrow it? "

" Borrow it? " Miss Furness echoed. " What for? "

" I'd like to sketch it. I might even make it part of an Oriental still life I want to paint. I'll be careful with it and return it to you next week." He looked from the slim green figure in his hands to Miss Furness and his bright smile flashed winningly. " I've never seen anything like this before. I'd like to see if I can catch its expression on paper."

Miss Furness hesitated. " Well — I suppose I'd rather have it out of the house until I've decided what to do with it. It must have some significance for my sister. But I shall hold you responsible for its safety, you know."

" I'll take care of it," Adrian promised. " I won't let Jill come anywhere near it."

Jill made a face at him, but this time she didn't mind his words. For once Adrian was just teasing her — like any other boy. Mostly, however, she was pleased that they could bring the cat home for a little while. Perhaps she and Andy could figure out why it had been hidden so carefully in the old bronze bell.

Hana joined them and she too exclaimed over the cat. When Miss Furness had gone back to her sister after still another warning to Adrian, Hana walked with them to the door. She was as fascinated by the cat as Jill was — probably because she had heard Miss Lydia bemoaning the loss of it for such a long time.

Just as they were saying good night and thanking her again for the dinner, Hana reached out and touched something just beneath the cat's pointed chin.

" Something around neck," she said.

Adrian turned the figure about in his hands. A fine strand of wire had been wound about its neck. Fastened to the wire, hanging down the back, was a narrow strip of thick, coarse paper, with Oriental characters written on it in black ink.

" Can you read what it says? " Andy asked Hana.

Hana lifted the strip with one finger to examine it more closely. Then she drew her hand away as if the paper had burned her.

" This is mos' bad thing," she said. " There is message."

" What do you mean ' a bad thing '? " Adrian asked. " What message? "

But Hana only shook her head. " Is hard for me to say. This character mean something bad."

" Maybe we can find someone who can read it," Andy said, and Hana's face lighted.

" I have friend in Chinatown — Lotus Wang. Father, Wang Fu, has shop on Grant Avenue. If cat is Chinese, is more better to ask Chinese about message. I will ask Lotus to help. Tomorrow I let you know."

So it was left at that and they went home to the Dallas house. Andy brought the book Miss Furness had lent them, while Adrian carried the green cat, trusting it to no one. At home he put it carefully on a high shelf in the bookcase, out of reach except from a footstool. He even put a heavy book in front of it, so it couldn't tumble off the shelf in the event of an earthquake. There had been no earthquakes since Jill's arrival, much to her disappointment, but Adrian said you could never tell.

Mother and Mr. Dallas wanted to hear all about the evening and were especially interested in the story of the green cat. Adrian listened too, though he held himself apart from the group.

It was funny about Adrian, Jill thought; sometimes when they were away from home he could be practically human. And he had tried to make up for his behavior that afternoon at the Coit Tower. But when he was home and Mother was present, he still looked scowly and sullen. And whenever he dared — though his father didn't like it — he returned to his game of pretending Mother wasn't there.

Tonight, however, he was interested in the story of the cat. And having met Miss Lydia, he stopped making unkind remarks about her.

" I think we ought to find out about that cat," he said to no one in particular. " If it's really a museum piece, as it could very well be, it's a shame to keep it shut up in that old house where no one can see it. Maybe Dad's friend at Gump's would know about it. Maybe I'll take it down to show him."

" I'll find you a box to wrap the cat in when you take it downtown," Mother offered. " Miss Furness would never forgive us if anything happened to it."

When she went to bed that night Jill had so many things to think about that she lay awake for a long while, listening to the night sounds. As it usually did

late on a summer afternoon, fog had crept in through
the Golden Gate and there were the usual warning
sounds from boats and horns and bells out on the bay.
Jill was getting so used to them now that most of the
time she scarcely heard them. But in the quiet hours of
the night all sound seemed to travel farther and become more distinct.

Principally, though, she thought about the cat mystery. Only yesterday it seemed to have reached a dead
end where no solution was possible. Now all sorts of
new things had opened up. The cat itself had been
found, though Miss Furness did not want her sister to
see it. Around the cat's neck was a strip of paper with
an ominous message which Hana's Chinese friend
might be able to translate. Perhaps the man at Gump's
would know more about the cat and where it had come
from. Then there was the book Andy had borrowed
from Miss Furness.

Jill had only dipped into it here and there so far. It
didn't look too promising, since it had been published
years before Karl von Wallenstein had been lost in
China. It was the account of an Indian expedition far
away from the home of the green cat. But since the
book was written by Miss Lydia herself it might be interesting. It would at least tell them what she had been
like as a young woman.

By now Jill's curiosity about the cat was not merely
because it was a baffling mystery. She had grown fond
of the little old lady who spent her life in a wheel chair
in the gloomy Furness house. No matter how good Miss
Matilda's intentions might be, she did keep her sister a

prisoner. And Jill couldn't help feeling that this was unfair and that Miss Lydia's life might be more satisfactory and interesting if she could be treated like other people. Maybe she ought to be shown the green cat and allowed to remember everything that had happened in connection with it.

For a few seconds Jill toyed pleasantly with make-believe in which she was the one to show Miss Lydia the cat, thus working everything out in a happy and satisfactory way. But she smiled at her own wish to play heroine, knowing she must not go against the wishes of Matilda Furness.

Now she thought again of the cat, of its queer dragon's snarl and its hollow eyes that somehow conveyed a feeling that it knew a great deal more than it was telling. Suddenly a thought struck her and Jill sat straight up in bed. Those eyes went through into nothing. So was the whole head, the whole cat, hollow inside? And if it were, could anything have been dropped through into the interior for safekeeping? In mystery stories the criminal was always taking the pearl necklace apart and dropping it bead by bead into some secret hiding place.

Jill listened intently — not to the outside noises now, but to the sounds within the house — to Carol's steady breathing in the next bed and to a long, steady snore from the boys' room. That was Andy, probably. She couldn't imagine Adrian being so human as to snore.

Quietly she slid her pajamaed legs over the side of the bed and stood up. Carol did not stir. A breeze through the open window was chill, and Jill scurried to the door, opened it softly and stepped into the little

hall. She couldn't wait till morning to satisfy her curiosity. Adrian would have a fit if she touched the cat —
but if she did it now he'd never know.

A wide patch of moonlight from the picture window
lighted the living room and she saw that the moon was
shining through wisps of fog. Her bare feet made no
sound on the floor as she carried a footstool over to the
bookcase. Then she climbed upon it and reached carefully for the cat. She held onto it tightly, stepped very
carefully to the floor.

At the window she raised the figure so that pale
moonlight touched it to life. The empty eyes were
black holes in a snarling, evil white face. Goodness, but
the thing looked spooky in this light with all the color
washed out of it! She could imagine the figure squirming to life in her hands, sinking those wicked teeth into
a finger. The thought made her clutch the cat all the
more tightly lest she frighten herself into dropping it.

Slowly she turned it about in the moonlight, but try
as she would, she couldn't see through the small slits
of the eyes into the head. It *was* hollow — she could
tell that. She shook the cat carefully up and down but
there was no interesting sound of something rattling
inside. Nobody had hid any pearls, or anything else,
here. There was nothing to do but give up her notion
of hidden treasure and set the cat back on its shelf. She
was glad enough to put it safely out of her hands and
scurry back to her warm bed.

Just as she stepped into the bedroom she heard something that made her pause and hold her breath — a
sound that was different out there in the night. *That*

wasn't a boat whistle or a foghorn. My goodness, was she getting to be like Miss Lydia?

She ran to the open window and stood beside it, forgetting about the chill of the San Francisco night. Far above on the hillside grotesque turrets shone through the fog where moonlight touched them. The house was pitch dark in all its windows. And yet — yes, there it was again! The sound of a bell ringing in the night. No electric bell with a steady hum, but a bell that clanged irregularly.

The sound came quite clearly from the direction of the Furness house on the hill. Someone — or something! — was ringing the temple bell in the curio room.

15

"THE EYES HAVE IT"

THE next morning Jill told Andy about the bell, but he only laughed at her.

"Look," he said, "you've got an imagination three times too big to make any sense. Nobody could ring that bell. It's grounded on the chest so it couldn't give a clear sound. And it's too heavy for anyone to handle alone. Unless it was suspended in some way it couldn't be rung. You were dreaming."

"I wasn't!" Jill cried. "I tell you I did hear that bell."

Andy only grinned. "You're getting as bad as Miss Lydia. Better not tell anybody else you heard it."

Jill could hardly restrain her impatience that morning. She was peeved with Andy. And there was nothing she could do but wait for something to happen. Hana had promised to phone Lotus Wang. Adrian was going to see the man at Gump's this afternoon. In the meantime there was absolutely nothing she could do to push anything ahead.

The cat sat regally on its high shelf and no one noticed that it had been moved during the night. Adrian, of course, was off to his art class, and Mother had taken Carol to a dancing lesson. Andy was building some mysterious project out on the back terrace — a contraption of wire and cork and bits of linoleum and chunks of metal. But since he was as touchy about his " inventions " as Adrian was when he was painting, Jill left him alone.

At least there was the book by Lydia von Wallenstein to be investigated. She settled down on the couch with it and began to read. This, it seemed, was an account of the first expedition the baron had made after Miss Lydia had married him. She spoke of her recent marriage and it seemed to have taken place some few years after the period described in *New Century in San Francisco*. Matilda had recovered from her illness by that time — so Lydia had been able to go on a trip with her husband.

She wrote about her plans to live in the Orient — possibly in Shanghai or in Yokohama in a few years. But at the time of this particular expedition, however, she and her husband were on a trip into India. Jill didn't read every word because she was skimming for information. In the Vale of Kashmir Miss Lydia had stayed with friends, while her husband went on past more difficult boundaries in the mountains. She wrote of the customs and people of the land while she waited for her husband's return.

It was interesting, but Jill found nothing that led toward what might have happened years later when Miss Lydia was much older and was living in a house in Yokohama.

The door chimes startled her from her reading and Jill flew to answer them. Her visitor was Hana and the Japanese girl explained breathlessly that she had talked on the phone to her Chinese friend. Lotus Wang would be happy to look at the characters around the cat's neck and see if she could translate them. If Jill wished, they could go to Chinatown now.

Jill glanced uncertainly at the cat, still high on the bookshelf. She didn't dare take it to Chinatown for Lotus to see.

Hana sensed her hesitation. " Is possible to remove wire from cat's neck. Lotus needs to see paper only."

So that was the way they managed it. Jill left a note for Mother on the kitchen table and she and Hana hurried to catch a bus for downtown. At Grant Avenue, the " Main Street " of Chinatown, they walked uphill on foot.

It was surprising how quickly one stepped from the Occident into the Orient on Grant Avenue. In one block there were the usual American shops. Then you crossed a street and the whole atmosphere, the very architecture, was different. Lampposts became Chinese lanterns and the roofs of some of the buildings had up-curving pagoda tops. Curio shops edged the sidewalk, those with expensive articles rubbing elbows with what Hana called " tourist junk." But even the " junk " looked fascinating to Jill.

Wang Fu, the father of Hana's friend, had a shop on Grant. It was larger than some of the others, with handsome show windows filled with robes of Chinese silk, porcelain objects, and fine jade jewelry. The aisles between the counters were wide and it was plain that this was a most superior shop.

Lotus sometimes helped her father in the store and she was waiting on a customer when the girls went in. She was a pretty girl, neatly dressed in a skirt and sweater, her black hair drawn back and held by a silver barrette. She had been born in San Francisco, Hana said, and had never been to China.

As soon as the customer left, Lotus came to greet the girls, her accent plainly American.

Hana explained about the finding of the green cat, and Lotus seemed fascinated by the story. When Jill took the strip of paper, carefully wrapped in tissue, from her pocket and gave it to her, Lotus examined it carefully. She not only went to a regular American school, she explained, but also attended Chinese classes and had learned the language and written characters of her father's country.

She shook her head soberly over the black ink writing on the slip of paper. Yes, indeed, Hana was right. " These are characters which mean bad fortune," she said. " But I don't know to whom, or whether they mean that the cat itself is bad luck. Just a moment — let me ask my father."

Mr. Wang came into the shop at his daughter's call. He greeted Hana pleasantly, and acknowledged the introduction to Jill. Lotus' father had come to the United States as a young boy and had attended an American university, so he too spoke without any trace of accent.

He examined the characters and gave his own opinion. " I don't believe these mean that the figure itself is bad luck," he said. " I would say that a threat of some sort is implied here to anyone who injures the cat, or who does not obey certain orders connected with it. The threat is very severe. The wrath of the gods is called down upon the offender."

" What orders do you mean? " Jill asked, more puzzled than ever.

Mr. Wang shook his head. " Perhaps there were more directions with this. The edge of the paper is rough — something could have been torn off. I cannot tell. Did you find nothing else in connection with it? "

" That's all there was," Jill said.

Mr. Wang was still examining the strip of paper. " There is something very curious about this. Please, Lotus, will you hand me the magnifying glass? "

Lotus picked up the glass from a desk and gave it to her father.

Again Mr. Wang studied the slip. " There seems to be some extraneous matter rather cunningly inserted around these characters — almost like a border on one side of the paper. But it is made up definitely of letters of the English alphabet. Do you see? "

Jill looked closely at the strip through the glass and saw what he meant. What she had indeed taken for a border were very tiny English letters. Perhaps someone had been trying to get a message through by using the green cat. She could make out a " T," then an " H " and an " E." Plainly the word, " THE." And there were a few more letters to be deciphered. Now that she knew they were there she could see them without

the glass. The message — if it were a message — was brief.

Now several customers came into the store chattering like summer tourists and exclaiming over some Chinese robes. Mr. Wang excused himself and went to wait on them, and Lotus accompanied Hana and Jill to the door.

When the girls had thanked her and said good-by, Jill turned quickly to Hana. " Let's go some place and figure this out."

" Portsmouth Square is near," said Hana. " We can sit on bench and talk. Also, this place in San Francisco is good for you to see."

It was fun to have such a lively, eager companion as Hana to share an adventure with, and Jill listened with interest as her friend talked on the way to the square.

" When I first come to this country," Hana said, " my father say I must learn about new home place. So he brings my mother and me around city, presenting all places of interest. Bery celebrated author in Portsmouth Square."

This was puzzling until Hana led the way down one of the paths that rayed toward the center of the square. Here graceful poplars made an arch above a small statue. On top of the pedestal sailed a golden galleon with all its sails puffed full with wind. Jill bent to read the inscription and found that this was the Robert Louis Stevenson monument. The ship represented the famous *Hispaniola* of *Treasure Island*.

" My father say," Hana explained, " this mos' famous author live one time in San Francisco. In this place he come to sit in shining sun and talk to sailors from many places."

Jill looked about her with new interest. How strange to think that Robert Louis Stevenson had walked upon this very ground! Today, however, there were no sailors in evidence. Chinese children played on the paths, and very old Chinese men sat on the benches watching them and dreaming. From Kearny Street came the continuous noise of traffic. Jill and Hana found a bench to themselves and once more Jill took the scrap of paper from her pocket.

Before they had left the shop Lotus had given them a sheet from a pad and a stubby pencil, so now they could write down the letters as they deciphered them. Soon there was a string that read: THEEYESHAVEIT. This was easily separated into: THE EYES HAVE IT. And it left them exactly nowhere. What eyes had what? And why did the Chinese characters carry all those threats of bad luck and curses from the gods?

Hana clapped one small hand over her mouth and jumped up from the bench. "Perhaps it is eyes of cat have something! Perhaps there is thing hiding inside."

"I already thought of that," Jill told her. "I even got up in the middle of the night and shook that cat good and hard to see if anything could have been dropped inside it through the eyes. If there was anything hidden in the cat, it's gone."

Hana sat down again, disappointed. But now Jill remembered something else about last night; something she had forgotten in her excitement over visiting Chinatown.

" Hana," she said earnestly, " did you hear anything queer in your house during the night? "

For a moment Hana's dark eyes widened and she looked almost fearful. Then she nodded solemnly.

" I hear bell," she said. " Bell ringing inside house. You think it is maybe ghost bell? "

Even in the sunshine of Portsmouth Square that was a shivery thought, but Jill dismissed it quickly. " No, of course not. But I'm glad you heard it too. Andy made fun of me. He said no one could have rung that temple bell."

" Bell rings in night," Hana said firmly.

Jill wondered if Miss Lydia had heard it too — much more plainly this time than in her imagination. And she wondered what Miss Lydia would make of these curious words about eyes on the strip of Chinese paper which had been fastened about the cat's neck. While Miss Furness had forbidden them to show her sister the cat, she had said nothing at all about this piece of paper.

" I know what I'd like to do right after lunch," Jill told Hana with new enthusiasm. " Do you think Miss Furness would mind if we brought Miss Lydia a bunch of flowers? "

Hana's eyes danced and Jill suspected she was once more enjoying herself as " mos' disobedient daughter."

" This is good idea," Hana said. " Frower stalls have many nice frowers."

Jill and Hana turned their pockets out and found that by pooling most of their money they would have enough for a fairly simple bouquet.

As they left Portsmouth Square, Hana explained more history to Jill. The square, she said, had been the old plaza around which the original San Francisco had been built. In the days of the vigilantes — whom Hana seemed to mix up in her mind with the long-ago samurai, the soldier nobles of Japan — there had even been executions of the wicked right here in the square.

At the moment, however, Jill was more interested in hurrying downtown to buy some flowers for Miss Lydia's bouquet. One of the things she loved about San Francisco were the gay flower stalls. At the first one they came to pails of blooms stood all around the stall on the sidewalk, while corsages and individual blossoms were laid out on shelves and trays. At the top the whole thing rose to a solid, banked mass of blossoms in bright yellow, blue, red, white and orange. The woman at the stall was friendly and helpful and they were able to fix up a dainty little bouquet for Miss Lydia.

They decided to finish the morning with a special treat, so they took a cable car that would carry them part way up Russian Hill. Luckily they found an outdoor seat at the front, where they could sit facing outward, clinging to poles that rose from step to roof. Behind them the gripman who ran the car manipulated the grip, which went through a slot in the pavement between the tracks to grasp a cable moving constantly beneath the street, pulling the car up the steepest of hills.

Off they went with a great crashing of gears and as they climbed the hill all the passengers had a tendency to slide sideways on the slippery wooden seats. At the turns the conductor shouted, " Hold on, turn! " and around the car swung with everyone clinging to the nearest pole. Sometimes Jill had a breathless feeling, looking back down a steep hill the car had just climbed. There were hills in San Francisco that were almost too steep to go up on foot.

Mother and Carol and Andy were home when Jill left Hana and went into the house. She put the flowers for Miss Lydia in a glass of water. Right after lunch she would take them to her. When Adrian came in, she told him about unwiring the strip of paper from about the cat's neck, and he was unpleasant about it. So unpleasant, in fact, that even Andy, who was usually patient with his twin, spoke up for her.

" Jill's not a baby. And she didn't hurt the cat. I think it was a good idea for her to take that paper to Chinatown."

" Just the same," Adrian said stiffly, " nobody is to touch the cat again. I'm the one who is responsible for its safety. For all we know, it may be worth thousands of dollars. I'll find out about that when I go down to see Mr. Gibbs this afternoon."

At lunch Jill told the others what Mr. Wang had said concerning the threat of the Chinese characters, but she said nothing in Adrian's presence about the English lettering. He was so smart — let him find that out for himself. But though she returned the paper to him to replace about the cat's neck, he didn't detect the tiny border writing at all, and Jill felt smugly superior about her knowledge.

When Adrian had gone downtown after lunch, Jill showed Andy her bouquet for Miss Lydia and asked him to come along to the Furness house.

" Count me in on the flowers too," he said. " Will a quarter help? I spent my allowance at the junk dealer's this week."

Jill accepted the offering and on the way uphill she told him about the words, " THE EYES HAVE IT."

" The cat's eyes! " said Andy at once, just like everyone else. " Maybe there's something inside."

So Jill had to confess what she had done during the night and make Andy promise not to tell Adrian.

Before they had a chance to ring, Hana opened the door. She had been watching for them and put a finger to her lips, beckoning them into the gloomy hall.

" Miss Furness takes nap upstairs," she whispered. " Walk with quiet, prease." But when they reached Miss Lydia's door Hana did not open it at once. Everything about her small person breathed excitement and secrecy as she came close to them, still whispering. " I have find something." She waved toward the curio room. " Before you go I show you."

Then she opened the door and there was no further chance to question her.

16

PAGES FROM A JOURNAL

HANA had told Miss Lydia she was to have visitors, and she had already rolled her chair into the sitting room to wait for them. Jill gave her the little bouquet and explained that it was from Hana, Andy, and herself.

Miss Lydia's hands shook a little as she took the cluster of white and pink and blue blossoms. She bent her silvery head to sniff the posies and when she looked up Jill saw tears in her bright-blue eyes.

" How lovely of you, children! Do pull up chairs and sit down and talk to me for a while. When I was a little girl I always loved surprises. I still love them. I don't suppose young people ever realize that there is still a very young person hiding inside most old people. For such a long, long time there have been no surprises in my life. Matilda takes good care of me, but she likes to do everything in exactly the same way every single day. She doesn't realize that a surprise now and then makes a person so much happier. Thank you, my dears."

This time it was Jill who sat upon the footstool

pulled close to Miss Lydia's knee. Since there was no
telling when there might be an interruption from Miss
Furness, she went to the main point of her visit right
away. Not even Andy knew what she meant to do and
he looked surprised when she spoke.

" Have you ever heard the words, ' the eyes have
it'? " Jill asked. " I mean in some special way that carried a meaning? "

Miss Lydia repeated the words and a faintly worried
look quirked her brows. " Eyes — eyes? I'm not sure.
I can't seem to remember. Oh, dear — if I could just
find my little green cat! "

It was Andy's turn to surprise Jill. " Why do you
want to find the cat? " he asked Miss Lydia quietly.
" How would it help you if you found the cat? "

Miss Lydia answered him in a perfectly normal, un-
mixed-up way. " Thank you for believing that there is
a cat. I've been treated like a child long enough. Matilda pooh-poohs the existence of the cat whenever I
mention it and tries to make me think I am dreaming.
But I know there was a cat. And I know it brought me
some sort of message. A message from Karl. But something happened — something dreadful happened. I
had to save the cat because it had a secret to tell me —
something terribly important."

" Was — was the dreadful thing an earthquake? "
Jill asked.

Miss Lydia's eyes brightened. " Of course! I remember now how frightful it was. The whole house shook
and jerked and things crashed all around me. But I
knew I had to save the cat."

She stopped and moved her hands vaguely, help-lessly, forgetting again.

" So perhaps you wrapped it up in newspaper and pieces of an old blanket," Jill said. " Perhaps you stuffed it inside that temple bell? "

Miss Lydia rubbed her fingers over her forehead. " With a severe earthquake there is always fire. My sister and I were here in this house when San Francisco burned, you know, following the '06 earthquake. But the time in Yokohama was even worse for me. I was alone in the house. Everyone ran into the streets, and I could hear people who were hurt screaming. But I knew the big bell would protect the cat. It couldn't be crushed and it wouldn't burn. It sat on a stone out in the garden, and when everything else burned it was not hurt at all."

" But why was it so important to save the cat? " Andy asked.

Miss Lydia shook her head in a worried way. " I don't know. I can't remember."

Before she could get lost in the fog that sometimes seemed to engulf her thoughts, Hana spoke breath-lessly.

"What is happening next? " she asked. " After earthquake? "

Miss Lydia recovered and went on quite naturally. " When I tried to leave the house a part of the roof collapsed and I was pinned in the wreckage. Some Japanese friends came to my aid and got me out. They took me into the country away from the wreckage of Yokohama, and I stayed until rescue ships came into the harbor and I could return to America. My friends got the bell for me and shipped it on the same boat, because I insisted on it. I was very ill. I could do nothing myself."

Miss Lydia was growing quite excited and upset now. The fog seemed to descend on her memory quickly, blotting everything out. She looked vaguely at Jill and Andy as if she did not even remember who they were.

Hana motioned to them. " More better you go now."

Miss Lydia put her hands over her face and did not look up. But as they went to the door, Jill heard her words clearly.

" The bell rang last night, I know I heard it. It is here — here in this house. If I could only remember — "

Hana pushed them into the hall. " Hurry, hurry! " she cried.

But her haste did not come soon enough. Just as they reached the front door, they heard Miss Furness calling from her room upstairs.

" Hana! Is that you, Hana? Is anyone there? "

" I come! " Hana called and opened the front door softly. Just before Jill and Andy went out she took several crumpled sheets of paper from a hiding place under the hall table and thrust them into Jill's hands. " Bell has old papers in stuffing," she whispered. " I find this — you keep."

She almost shoved them out the door, and hurriedly closed it behind them.

" Let's get out of here," said Andy and they ran down the steps together. Jill didn't dare look back to see if Miss Matilda Furness watched them from an upper window. This time she might really be angry.

Not until they were well out of sight of the house did Jill stop and hold up the few pages of blue-lined copybook paper Hana had thrust into her hands. Hana must have smoothed them out as best she could, but they had been wadded into wastepaper and were crinkled into hundreds of tiny lines.

" Looks like they were ripped from a notebook," Andy said, noting the rough tear along one side of each sheet. " What's all that pen writing say? "

It was hard to tell because of the crinkles, because the ink had faded to some extent, and the penmanship was barely legible.

" I can't make out enough words to read it," Jill said doubtfully. She turned over a sheet. " Look — there's a date — and the word ' Yokohama.' Maybe Miss Lydia was keeping a journal and tore it up after the earthquake to make more stuffing for the bell."

" What's that funny thing? " Andy said, pointing at the page in her hand.

A crude diagram had been drawn on the paper.

" Are they flower petals? " Jill puzzled.

Andy shook his head. " Looks more like a batch of eyes. Anyway let's take these home and ask Dad about them tonight. He's good at figuring out handwriting."

They decided to let it go at that and went straight home. Adrian was there ahead of them, looking glum and disgusted.

" Didn't you see the man at Gump's? " Andy asked.

" Sure I saw him. It didn't take him two minutes to

decide about the cat. He said it was a rather crude, fairly modern piece. Interesting, but without any value."

Jill felt no disappointment. She didn't believe that the importance of the cat rested on its value as an art piece.

"What did you do with the cat?" Jill asked.

Adrian shrugged. "Oh, it's around somewhere. I guess I tossed it on the sofa."

Jill found the figure quickly and picked it up. Once more she felt indignant with Adrian. "Just because it doesn't interest you any more, doesn't mean you need to be careless with it. Miss Furness still doesn't want it broken."

"She won't care when I tell her it's not worth anything," Adrian said. "Anyway, you're not so smart as a detective. If you used your head — "

Jill broke in on his taunt. " It looks just as queer and interesting to me as it did in the first place! " she insisted. " Yesterday you wanted so badly to paint it. And it's still the same piece." She held the cat up for Adrian to see. " Look at that wicked green face! Why don't you go ahead and paint it anyway? "

In spite of himself, Adrian's interest returned. " Maybe you're right. I suppose I ought to make some sketches anyway, before I take it back uphill."

He went to work at once, and Andy returned to his latest invention out on the terrace. The new contraption was not turning out the way he wanted it to, and he was now tearing it down for the third time. When Jill looked out a window later that afternoon and saw her mother on the terrace talking solemnly to Andy, she felt unexpectedly warm and comfortable.

She could remember the pang of resentment she had felt that day at the airport, when Mr. Dallas had driven them here for the first time and Mother sat with Andy in the back seat. But now Jill could only feel happy and satisfied to see them together. Mother had tried so hard with the boys, and she deserved the sort of shy friendship Andy was beginning to give her. Of course he had been the nice one from the start, but now he was more than just polite. He was accepting Mother as someone he liked and trusted.

The afternoon was difficult to kill because now Jill was impatient for Mr. Dallas to come home so she and Andy could consult him about those pages from the journal. More than once she tried to decipher the words again, but while she could figure out a snatch here and there, the writing had been carelessly hasty, as though the writer's thoughts were flying faster than her fingers.

Jill wondered if this had been the way Miss Lydia wrote her books in manuscript form. Or perhaps made notes for them in journal form. Anyway Roger could figure it all out.

" Roger! " There, she had said his name in her own mind. But she still felt self-conscious about saying it out loud.

At mealtime these days there was so much to talk about that Adrian and his silences were often forgotten. Between them at dinner Jill and Andy poured out the day's adventures and even recounted their visit with Miss Lydia. Mother and Mr. Dallas were increasingly interested.

Mother said, " Let's leave the dishes and have a look at those pages right after dinner." This was a most satisfactory course of action and only Adrian remained aloof. He opened the piano and stared at it moodily. Now and then he moved his hands over the keys as if he were playing music that only he could hear. And once in a while he actually plunked a key. But no one paid much attention to him because Mr. Dallas, magnifying glass in hand just like Mr. Wang, was hot on the trail of what those scribbled words really said.

They were sad words, mostly, and they were plainly Miss Lydia's. She had written them some months after Karl von Wallenstein had gone into China never to be heard from again. Some of the passages had obviously been written by a woman who was lonely and brokenhearted. Mr. Dallas said they were private and shouldn't be read by others, so he skipped over them.

At the piano Adrian plunked the C keys all the way up from bass to treble and then plunked them down again. No one looked at him. All but Carol were too busy watching Mr. Dallas, waiting for any revelation he might make. Carol sat on the floor, cutting out paper dolls. When Adrian plunked the keys she hummed the notes up and down the scale right along with him.

Mr. Dallas' magnifying glass paused in its course across the paper and he looked up at them, interested and excited. " Here we are! I think we've found something now. Listen to this."

He read the words aloud slowly, puzzling out the hard ones as he went along. The account told of the way the figure of the green cat had been brought from hand to hand out of the interior of China and delivered to a friend of Karl's in Shanghai. Not the details, of course, but that this had happened. The friend had obeyed instructions to deliver the cat to Karl's wife in Japan.

It is of no intrinsic value [Miss Lydia had written], but it tells me that Karl was alive when it was sent and I treasure it for that reason. I am informed that the Chinese characters on the strip wired about the cat's neck call down the vengeance of the gods upon any who interfere with the cat's delivery to its destination. Of course this was Karl's way of insuring that it would reach me, even though it must pass through many ignorant hands.

There was a break and a tiny sputter of ink at that point, as though emotion had caused the hand of the writer to waver. Then the passage went on.

Karl *must* be alive! I knew they were wrong when they told me he had probably been murdered like his partner. It has been six months since they found the body of Fred Parke. But the Chinese loved Karl and they never trusted Fred. Karl himself did not trust him. I know they quarreled. I know what Fred was like. Karl would never have gone with him on another trip had it not been necessary.

Once Karl drew me a caricature of Fred Parke that looked like this. [Here the drawing Jill and Andy had noted was inserted.] The picture portrayed an eye in the middle and a circle of small eyes all looking inward at the centered one. That was Fred, Karl said. An enormous self-centered eye, with the vanity of all those other eyes looking in upon himself. Good people, generous people, look outward at least some of the time. But Fred had always to be the center of all attention and all publicity. How many times in the past he took credit for what Karl had done! Not that Karl minded. He cared less than I did, being wrapped up in the work itself. I would like to tell the truth in the next book I write. But I cannot tell it when I do not know how Fred died, or the final thing that happened.

A line was skipped and a new date written in. The journal went on.

Someone has been circulating an ugly story lately to the effect that the trouble between Karl and Fred rose to such a pitch that Fred died at my husband's hands and was not killed by bandits. It is even said that Karl has disappeared on purpose, so as not to face the charge of murder. What utter nonsense! What wicked lies! If only I could answer them and clear his name! Fortunately this is no more than local spite gossip here in Yokohama's foreign colony.

Then at a still later date:

Has the cat some special significance, I wonder? Is it supposed to tell me something? I have the growing feeling that it is. Today I examined it again very closely and I discovered something. Something which escaped me before. English letters, very tiny, have been printed in a sort of border design beside the Chinese characters. Karl must have felt that a letter would not be sent through native hands with reasonable hope that it would reach its destination from wherever he was — I am sure in bandit hands. But this figure with a curse upon it might get through. So he sought to send me a message with the cat.

I have deciphered the letters and they read very plainly: THE EYES HAVE IT. I have been puzzling over that ever since. Have these words something to do with Fred Parke and Karl's caricature of the eyes? It is possible. But so far I have not been clever enough to figure out the meaning. I can write no more now. I am too sad and discouraged and tired.

There were only a few paragraphs more about inconsequential matters, written another time. Then the page ended and there was no more.

" So that's what the reference to eyes means," Andy said. " Something to do with that partner, Fred Parke. I'll bet she put these pages in with the cat to explain about it if it fell into somebody else's hands."

" Do you think Karl von Wallenstein could still be alive? " Jill asked hopefully.

Mr. Dallas shook his head. " You must remember that these pages were written nearly thirty-five years ago. So I think that's hardly possible. Where is the cat,

Jill? Let me have a look at it."

Adrian had been sketching the figure and he went to get it from his studio, handed it to his father. Then he returned to thumping the piano, to show he had no interest in what was going on.

But though Mr. Dallas shook the cat vigorously, nothing fell out, nothing rattled inside. Andy, who had been looking thoughtful, suddenly clapped a hand to the side of his head.

" Gosh, am I a dope! Jill — remember when we were looking through those newspapers at the library? We skipped all the Sunday magazine section stuff because it was all about scandals and buried treasure and murders."

" You said it was no use to spend time reading through all that," Jill said.

" That's why I'm a dope. What if this story that was going around Yokohama appeared in the San Francisco papers? Something must have happened to make Miss Furness decide she'd have nothing more to do with reporters. Maybe this was it."

Adrian played several loud chords dramatically and swung about on the bench. " Of course it was! I told Jill she wasn't so hot as a detective or she'd have thought of it. I went to the library a while back and had a look at those Sunday papers myself."

17

ANDY TAKES A HAND

Everyone stared at Adrian. Even Carol paused as she was cutting out the picture of a ballet dancer, her scissors in the air. Adrian, looking superior, turned back to the piano.

" Well, for goodness' sakes," Jill cried, " why didn't you say something? "

Adrian shrugged. " Nobody asked me. And you were all so smart. Why should I tell you anything? "

Without any warning Mr. Dallas exploded suddenly and thoroughly.

" We've all had enough of your rudeness! " he said sharply to Adrian. " Emily has gone out of her way to be sweet to you. She has defended you and sympathized with your feelings. She has even kept me from bawling you out as you deserved. And Jill has tried to be friendly in spite of how you've pushed her away. From now on I want to see a change. Otherwise you and I are going to have a serious session together."

There was a moment of frozen silence, while they stared at Roger Dallas and tried not to look at Adrian. Then Mother put a light, restraining hand on her husband's arm and spoke gently to Adrian.

" Please tell us what you found out," she said.

Adrian's face had turned a bright scarlet. His voice was very low as he answered.

" It — it was a pretty mean story with big headlines: IS KARL VON WALLENSTEIN A MURDERER? There was an exaggerated drawing in the middle of the page, with slant-eyed Chinese peering out of a bamboo thicket and one white man shooting another."

He paused, took a deep breath, glanced at his father's stern face, and then went on.

" There were photographs too — of Karl and his partner, and of Lydia von Wallenstein and her sister, Matilda Furness. There was even a sketch of that house up the hill and a heading: WHAT EVIL MYSTERY HIDES IN THIS MANSION? "

" But what did the piece say? " Jill urged.

" Nothing much, really," Adrian admitted. " Mostly it just asked questions and speculated. But it threw plenty of suspicion on Karl von Wallenstein and implied that his wife knew the truth."

" How dreadful! " Mother said. " No wonder Miss Furness was upset and wouldn't talk to any more reporters. As if her poor sister hadn't been through enough already! "

Adrian had recovered a bit and was trying to act as if nothing had happened. " What if the story was really true? What if Miss Lydia found out more than she told before she left Japan? Her journal sounds as though she was trying to find out whatever she could."

Both Andy and Jill went loyally to Miss Lydia's defense, but Adrian merely shrugged again.

" It's nothing to me," he said. " I don't see what difference it makes anyway. This story was dead and buried many years ago. All that's left is a couple of queer
old ladies up the hill."

" And the green cat," Andy said quietly. " Maybe
the cat is the one who knows the true story."

That was an odd thing to say and for a moment they
all stared at the figure in Mr. Dallas' hands.

But the important thing, Jill felt, was the fact that
Miss Lydia was still very much alive and for that reason — for her sake and her comfort — the mystery
ought to be worked out and not buried.

" When you're ready to return the cat to Miss Furness, let me take it to her," Jill said to Adrian. " You
aren't worried any more about its getting broken, are
you? "

" I guess not," Adrian said.

His father gave the cat back to him silently, and he
went to his painting as if he were eager to be alone.
But he didn't say whether or not he would let Jill return the figure to Miss Furness.

For a few days it seemed as though Mr. Dallas' outburst had cleared the air. Adrian behaved much more
amiably, on the surface at least. It was almost as though
he knew he had a scolding coming and was relieved to
be pulled up short and set on another course. He was
unusually courteous to Mother and stopped trying to
pretend she wasn't there. Nevertheless, Jill had a feeling that the change wasn't permanent.

Now he had started playing the piano again, and for
some reason the music made Jill uneasy. She read some

of the titles on the music rack and found they were pieces by Tchaikovsky, Schubert, and Mozart — all classical music. It seemed to Jill that he played very well, but everything he touched sounded mournful.

Andy and Jill checked up on the Sunday paper story at the library, but they learned nothing Adrian hadn't already told them. It was a horrid write-up and Jill could imagine how Miss Lydia must have felt if she had seen that cruel drawing. But there was no real answer to be found and it began to seem again that the mystery of the green cat had been worked out as far as possible.

That left Jill thoroughly dissatisfied. There were too many unfinished ends that hung dangling. Too many unanswered questions. The only move left was to show the cat to Miss Lydia and see if the sight of it brought back memories. But that was the very thing Miss Furness seemed determined not to do. Of course there was still the strange matter of the bell. Though Jill listened for it several times, she did not again hear it ringing in the house up the hill.

One afternoon when Adrian was at the piano again, Andy stalked in from the rear terrace with grease all over his hands and an angry look on his face. Jill had curled up on the sofa to read a book about old San Francisco, and Carol, who was happily unconcerned with emotional undercurrents, was dancing to Adrian's music. Carol was the one person Adrian never seemed to snap at, or be unkind to. That at least was to his credit.

Now, to Jill's astonishment, Andy went straight to

the piano and laid one greasy hand over the music sheets in front of his brother.

" Why don't you lay off? " he asked. " You always said you liked modern music. So why do you play things you've always been snooty about? "

" You know very well why! " Adrian snapped. " And take your greasy paw off that music."

Andy didn't budge. " Yes, I know why. These are pieces that were Mom's favorites. You're trying to hurt everybody in this house by playing them. But the only fellow you're really hurting is you! "

With both hands Adrian made an angry, crashing sound on the piano keys and pushed the bench back to stand up. Carol, frightened for once, scooted over to burrow into a corner of the couch beside Jill. For a moment Jill thought Adrian was going to hit his brother, but Mother heard the commotion and came to the kitchen door.

" Boys, boys! " she cried. " Whatever is the matter? "

Andy was watching Adrian and his face was red with anger. Jill was sure there would be an awful fight if Adrian made one move toward his twin.

Mother came up behind Andy and put her hands gently, affectionately on his shoulders, and beneath her touch he seemed to relax a little. The anger went slowly out of him, though he still regarded Adrian indignantly. Adrian stood quite still, very proud and distant and alone. Mother must have sensed his aloneness.

" You know, boys," she said quietly, " the thing I've felt best about, ever since I came here to live, is the affection between you two. I know all brothers have

spats sometimes, but I like the way you twins stick together. We mustn't let anything hurt that seriously."

Adrian made a scornful sound that denied any liking for anyone, but Mother went on quickly.

" I hope you'll both feel better by dinnertime because I'm planning a surprise for tonight. Your father
is going to be away at a dinner meeting, so we're going
to have a little party by ourselves. Let's make it a happy
time."

Andy recovered himself and smiled at Mother over
his shoulder. " Sure, Emily," he said. " That'll be
swell."

Adrian said nothing. He took the sheets of music
carefully from the rack and put them away in the
bench. Then he went back to his painting behind
the screens. Jill followed her mother worriedly into the
kitchen.

" Is this going to be the shish kebab dinner? " she
asked.

Mother nodded. " I know how to make it perfectly
now. And it's best to have it while Roger is away because Adrian has a feeling that his father is being critical of him these days. I'd rather serve it when his father isn't watching. I have a notion that if I can really
please Adrian and get him to trust me, everything will
be better."

Jill watched the approach of the dinner hour uneasily. When Mother called and the two boys sat down to
the table Adrian didn't look in a partyish mood.

Mother had kept everyone but Jill out of the kitchen
and after they had tomato soup and crackers, Jill helped

bring in the vegetables. Mother was taking the shish kebab out from under the broiler. Long skewers held pieces of lamb and vegetables. The kebabs were browned just right and smelled delicious. Jill carried in the cauliflower with cheese sauce, and baked potatoes bursting fluffy white through brown skins and topped by lusciously melting butter.

" M'm, yummy! " said Carol. " But where's the surprise? "

" Hold the door open, somebody," Mother called and Andy went to hold the swinging door. Dramatically Mother came into the room, carrying the platter high in her hands. She set it down on the table with a little flourish and Jill saw her turn almost pleadingly to Adrian.

Adrian, however, was not looking at Mother. He stared at the big platter with its skewers of meat as if he couldn't believe his eyes.

Andy said, " Well, look at this! " and sat quickly down to the table, making smacking sounds with his lips, clinking his silverware, as if he wanted to take Mother's attention away from Adrian.

Mother began to serve and she fixed Adrian's plate first. He didn't say anything as she set it before him, but he did not look like someone happily surprised.

" I — I found a cookbook of foreign recipes," Mother explained, plainly dismayed by the way Adrian was taking this. " The kebab recipe sounded interesting, so I've been practicing it. I do hope I've got it right."

She went on serving the others and then picked up her fork to start eating. Adrian did not reach for his.

He made a sound as though he were choking as he got up from the table and went out of the room. They could hear the bedroom door close, hear the sound of a key turned in the lock.

Mother looked at Andy, her cheeks pink. " I — I've done the wrong thing, haven't I? "

Stanchly Andy shook his head. " Not for me. Boy, I sure like this stuff." He picked up his fork, but he lidn't try to eat right away. To Jill's distress she saw tears in Andy's eyes.

" Tell me what's wrong! " Mother said, sounding very humble and young, so that Jill yearned to comfort her.

Andy gulped. " I — I don't like to tell you. But the last time we had this dish was the day — the day Mom died."

Mother looked shocked. " How terrible! Why didn't your father tell me? "

" Dad wasn't home that night — he wouldn't know what we had," Andy said. " We ate Sunday dinner at two o'clock and she fixed this for just the three of us because it was one of our favorites. She'd been sick on and off for a couple of years, but we didn't know she wasn't feeling well that day. Then later — in the evening — " He stopped and there was no need for him to go on.

Mother pushed her plate aside and put her head down on the table and wept. She hid her face in the crook of her arm and cried little choking sobs that were heartbreaking to hear. Carol ran to her, hugging her and crying too. Jill didn't know what to do. She could remember her mother crying once a long time ago, after Daddy had died. But not again, at least not when they could see. She felt sick with worry and helplessness.

Andy pushed his chair back and went out of the house to the back terrace. When Jill heard noises coming from outside, she got up to look out the window. Andy was doing a very queer thing. He had picked up a hammer and he was smashing his " invention " absolutely flat. She waited until there was nothing recognizable left of it and then she spoke to him through the window. It seemed as though the only important thing at the moment was to get everyone back on an ordinary everyday course.

" Don't you think we'd better eat dinner? " she said. " It's getting cold."

Andy stared at her, his face still red from his effort. Then the hammer dropped from his hand. Smashing the thing had evidently served its purpose. Jill suspected that he had smashed a lot of unhappy feelings right out of him. Now he grinned at her in a lopsided way.

" Sure," he said. " I'm hungry."

So Mother sopped up her tears and became herself again, apologizing for her behavior. Andy, Carol, Jill, and Mother sat down to eat the cooling shish kebab and it really was delicious. Even Andy ate with an appetite, so they finished up Adrian's share too. Mother said she would fix him something else later on and take it to his room.

But when she carried a tray to his door, he wouldn't let her in.

18

RETURN OF THE GREEN CAT

THE next day Adrian said nothing about what had happened. He went right on acting as he had before — which meant that he was thoroughly unpleasant and un-co-operative. In the afternoon he went out to sketch, but before he left he tossed the green cat carelessly in Jill's lap.

"You can take it back, if you want to," he said.

Jill managed to catch the cat without dropping it. Adrian was the limit. Just because he didn't think it had any value didn't mean he had any right to be careless with it. This was something Miss Lydia had treasured because her husband had sent it to her and it had reached her after he was probably dead in China. If Miss Furness should decide to show it to her sister, it must certainly be in good shape.

"Come with me to return it," she said to Andy, and he agreed readily.

As they climbed the hill together, Jill carrying the cat with the utmost care, Andy began to speak haltingly about his brother.

"I don't know what to do about him," he said.

" Sometimes I feel as though I'd have to fight him one of these days. But I don't want to do that. I wish you could have known him the way he used to be. He was such a — a bright sort of boy."

" You mean bright-shiny, don't you? " Jill said. " I know. I felt that the very first time I saw him. But he didn't back it up."

" He's changed so much he's like a different person. But you know something — I don't think he likes being different."

" Maybe not," Jill said. " I suppose he just doesn't know how to turn around. I feel like that sometimes too. I do something I know is wrong and then I have to keep doing more wrong things because I can't get turned back. But something has to turn Adrian around. It's too awful this way."

" I expect," said Andy gloomily, " that I'll have to beat him up pretty soon."

That didn't sound like a very good solution to Jill, but now they had reached the Furness house and she forgot about Adrian.

Hana let them in and Miss Furness herself came to the railing of the second floor gallery that ran above the central hall. " Who is it? " she called. " Oh — the children from down the hill? "

" We've brought something back," Jill said cautiously. She didn't want to say " cat " out loud, lest Miss Lydia hear.

Matilda Furness leaned toward them on the rail. " I see. Well, leave it on the hall table and come upstairs, both of you. I want to talk to you."

Jill and Andy glanced at each other. This was the first time they had been invited upstairs in this house. Jill set the cat down on the table.

Hana waved them toward the stairs, but she did not follow them up. Miss Furness invited them into her upstairs sitting room. The day was a little chill and she had a cheerful fire burning in the grate, but the room had a stuffy smell that made Jill long to open a window on some good fresh air.

Unlike Miss Lydia's room downstairs, this was the most cluttered place Jill had ever seen. It was not untidy — just filled to the brim with odd pieces of furniture, knickknacks, sofa cushions embroidered with everything from Indian heads to canoeing scenes, and other oddities from the past. Jill tried to be polite and not stare, but Andy's eyes were fairly popping.

" Sit down, do," said Miss Furness. She looked quite severe and ironclad today, just as she had the very first time Jill had seen her.

Jill and Andy seated themselves on a black horsehair sofa. The stuff was slippery and it prickled Jill's legs beneath the hem of her skirt. Andy wriggled and his elbow struck something on a table nearby. It teetered and fell off on the floor with a loud metallic clang that made Jill jump. She stared at the thing that had clattered to Andy's feet and saw that it was a bell. Quickly she reached for it, picking it up before Andy could do so. It was an odd-looking bell a few inches high, with square corners — not at all Oriental in appearance.

" That's a cowbell from Switzerland," Miss Furness said stiffly.

Jill had to ask the question that came to her mind. " Did you ever ring this bell? I mean late at night? "

For once Miss Matilda looked faintly flustered. " So you heard me? Yes, I did. I got to thinking about the way my sister keeps remembering a bell, and I wondered if hearing a real bell ring would mean anything to her."

" But we thought you didn't want her to remember," Andy put in.

Unexpectedly Miss Furness twisted her hands together in a gesture of despair. " Lately I haven't been sure what was right. I must admit that my sister has seemed better and I began to wonder if I ought to help her to remember everything."

" She has already remembered about the bell," Jill said. " She told us she packed the green cat in the bell at the time of the earthquake."

Miss Matilda was taken aback. " Oh, indeed? " She took the bell from Jill's hands and set it on a marble-topped table. " I have begun to feel that Lydia's improvement has been partly due to your visits. I know you are only children, but she has always had a fondness for the young."

She sighed and looked at Jill and Andy as if she were trying to figure out how anyone could like a child.

" Perhaps I've been wrong to try to protect Lydia from the world as I have," she went on, pondering to herself. " When we were young she was completely devoted to me. She even postponed her marriage in order to take care of me for a time when I was ill. I owe her a great deal. After she came home to me an invalid something very dreadful happened and I decided that at all costs she must be protected from those who tried to hurt her."

" You mean that old story in the Sunday paper? " Andy said.

Miss Furness looked at him sharply. " You don't miss a thing, do you? " But one mouth corner went up a little, so she wasn't angry. " Yes — that was a wicked attack upon poor Karl. Lydia saw the story before I could prevent it. It wasn't that she had not heard the rumors before, but to have it appear in print like that in this country was devastating. The reporters and the idly curious began to torment her. She had no answer to the suspicions, her health was at a low ebb and she collapsed in a complete breakdown. During the months that I nursed her all these unhappy things slipped out of her conscious mind. It seemed better that way and I shut the world away from her so she wouldn't remember."

She paused and gave Jill and Andy a suddenly surprised look.

" Gracious! I don't know why I'm explaining all this to you two children."

Jill ignored that. " Sometimes she remembers about the green cat, doesn't she? "

" Yes. And she speaks of it more and more lately. But I don't think she will recall the terrible accusation against her husband unless she sees the cat again. What will happen if she remembers completely, I don't know. It may be too much for her to bear. That is why I wanted to talk to you — though I didn't mean to go into so much detail. I thought if you knew the general story, you might continue to see her, but be very careful to keep away from dangerous subjects until I decide what to do. Are you old enough to understand this? "

" We aren't babies," said Jill, a little tired of all this criticism of being young.

Again the smile quirked one corner of Miss Furness' mouth. " I apologize for my doubts. Now if you'd like to run downstairs and see my sister, I'm sure she would be happy for a visit."

The interview was at an end and the two hurried out of the stuffy room, glad enough to escape. Of the two sisters, Jill certainly preferred Miss Lydia.

Their visit with Lydia von Wallenstein that afternoon was one of the pleasantest they'd had. Hana was there too, and after a while Miss Matilda joined them. But for once she sat quietly in a chair by the window crocheting a lace table runner, not breaking into the talk.

Miss Lydia was in a cheerful, remembering mood — though her memories did not deal with the unhappy. She had experienced so many adventures in her life and she could tell about them entertainingly. It was a shame she no longer wrote books, Jill thought. Such stories would make wonderful books.

She was well into an account of a tiger hunt she and Karl had gone on in India, when the startling thing happened. Jill felt the floor shake under her very feet. The uneasy sensation lasted no more than a second or two before it stopped. She glanced at Andy with startled eyes and he laughed out loud.

" It's only an earthquake," he said. " A very little one. You've been wanting to feel one — and you don't even know what it is when it happens."

Jill started to speak, but Hana uttered a sound of distress. She was staring at Miss Lydia and Jill saw that their friend sat straight up in her wheel chair, her fingers gripping the arms, her color a gray pallor.

" That was the first shock," Miss Lydia said between tight lips. " There will be more. Don't go out in the street — there'll be flying tiles from the roof tops. Stand under a door beam — that's the safest place. Until the fire comes. The fire will take everything! "

There were few tiles on San Francisco roofs. Miss Lydia must think she was back in Japan.

Miss Matilda reached her sister and put quieting hands on her shoulders as she tried to rise from her chair.

" It's all right, dear. That was only a small tremor. It's over and we're perfectly safe."

But Miss Lydia, frail as she was, struggled fiercely in her sister's hands. " The cat! My little green cat! I've got to save it. Bring it to me at once — bring me the little green cat! "

The command was so earnest, so forceful, that Jill jumped to her feet and looked anxiously at Miss Matilda. Matilda Furness threw up her hands in a despairing gesture and nodded to Jill.

" Go get it. Bring it to her."

Jill flew into the hall. The cat had toppled over on the hall table, but it was unharmed and she snatched it up, ran back to Miss Lydia's room. In her haste and her

eagerness, she forgot all her previous caution and care.
She forgot about the doorsills in old houses. Her toe
struck the sill and she went sprawling into the room on
her hands and knees. Out of her hands flew the cat,
bouncing across the room to crash against the iron
grate of the fireplace.

Hana cried, " Mah, mah! " in dismay, but Miss Matilda and Andy were too shocked to utter a sound. Miss
Lydia stared for an instant at the shattered base of the
cat which had rolled to her feet. Then she put her
hands over her face.

Jill got shakily to her feet and went over to the fireplace. The head of the cat, with its snarling mouth and
pointed ears, had been smashed completely. The rest
was in bits all over the floor. The only big piece left
was the lower fourth of the figure, broken off in a
chunk from the rest.

Miss Matilda burst into angry words of reproach
that were not pleasant to hear. Jill tried to shut the
sound out, poking helplessly at the green base of the
figure with one toe. She was surprised when Andy came
suddenly to her aid.

" Anybody could stub a toe," he defended Jill. " It
wasn't her fault. It might have happened to — to anybody! "

" I — I'm sorry," Jill said mournfully to Miss Lydia.
" I meant to be so careful and — and then — "

Miss Lydia took her hands from before her face. She
drew a very deep breath and then managed a wavery
smile.

" It's all right, Jill dear. Hand me that little piece of
my cat, will you please? "

Jill picked it up and gave it to Miss Lydia. She felt so awful that she didn't know which way to turn. There wasn't any excuse for what had happened and she had done irreparable damage. All she wanted was to go off

by herself where she needn't face anybody, to hide until somehow she managed to live through this awful experience.

Andy left his chair to look over Miss Lydia's shoulder. " That's funny," he said in an odd voice. " Isn't there something stuck down inside that base? Some sort of brown stuff? "

Miss Matilda stopped her reproaches and they all

crowded about Miss Lydia's chair. With trembling fingers Miss Lydia poked into the hollow of the base. Slowly, slowly, she began to pull something out. Jill reached to help her and found that a narrow strip of stiff reddish-brown paper had been curled round and round in the base of the figure until it was wedged in so tightly that nothing could have made it rattle or fall out.

19

OUT OF THE PAST

"I DO believe this is protective paper from a roll of film," Miss Lydia said, running it through her fingers. " Not the film — just a long thin strip cut from the wrapping. See — it's black on one side, brown on the other."

" It's narrow enough to be poked through the hollow eyes of the cat! " Jill cried, bending closer. " And there's writing on it. It's faint, but it really is writing! "

They all but banged heads trying to look at the strip at the same time.

" It has been written with an indelible pencil," Miss Matilda said. " Since you children have good eyes — what does it say? "

Fortunately this writing was not as undecipherable as Miss Lydia's in her journal pages. Jill could read it quite easily. She slid the long strip through her hands as she read aloud to the room. Andy helped her whenever she got stuck.

It was clear that these words had been written long ago by Karl von Wallenstein. Jill could feel shivers go down her spine and she didn't dare look at the others in the room. The thing was almost creepy — a voice speaking to them out of the long ago past.

We have been taken by bandits.

Those were the first words. The account was jerky, as if Karl had to write in secret and only in snatches. But it was all here.

He said that most of the native bearers had fled the week before. The party had been trying to go ahead with those left. But they had been captured and were now being marched into the wild interior. Karl had managed to keep on good terms with the bandit chief by making promises of ransom.

" It must have been more than that," Miss Lydia said gently. " Karl understood the Chinese. He knew several dialects and he could make friends with anyone. It wouldn't be just the promise of money that won liking for him."

Jill read on, now and then stumbling over a word. Fred Parke had not had Karl's gift for friendship. He had angered the bandit leader, who had shot him and continued the march, leaving his body behind.

Miss Lydia looked up at her sister. " You see! I knew it was something like that. Now we must call the reporters in and clear Karl's name of that dreadful story." She was remembering everything quite clearly now. " What else, Jill? "

The words grew harder to read. Karl wrote that he was ill. The medicine kit had been lost. The Chinese were kind to him, but he was growing worse. They had stopped in a small village where the people were forced to pay money to the bandits for " protection."

Karl had a plan for getting a message out. There was

a fellow here who made crude but interesting china figures. It might work — he was going to try. . . . He sent all his love and devotion to his wife Lydia. The name " Karl von Wallenstein " was scribbled shakily on the paper. And then nothing. There was more paper, but nothing else had been written on it. In all probability Karl had died of his illness after sending off the message.

Tears shone in Miss Lydia's eyes, but she held out her hands to Jill. " If you had not fallen, if you had not dropped my little cat, we might never have known about this. I remember now — the outside slip said, ' The eyes have it,' but I didn't understand and there never seemed to be anything inside. I can never thank you enough, Jill my dear."

It was strange to be elevated so suddenly and unexpectedly to the role of heroine. Especially when all she had done was to fall clumsily on her nose. Jill felt happy and tremendously relieved, but still a little dizzy.

" I think," said Miss Matilda, all the crossness gone from her voice, " that my sister has had enough excitement for one day. Perhaps you had better go now. Though you must come again, of course."

" But the reporters! " Miss Lydia cried. " I must talk to the press at once! "

" Lydia dear," Miss Matilda said, " you must realize that this story is years old by now. No one remembers any more. It no longer matters."

" Of course it matters! " Miss Lydia insisted. " Karl's name must be cleared. I must find a way to clear it! "

She was growing excited and Andy spoke to her awkwardly. " Of course I've got to talk to Dad first. But this seems like an awfully good story. It might be that he could write it up for his newspaper. With some pictures, maybe, and — and an interview."

" Of course," said Miss Lydia. " That's the way to do it. You must go home at once and tell him." She all but shooed them from the room in her anxiety to hurry this along.

Hana took them to the door as usual and chattered her own excitement all the way. " Is most wonderful! You are very crever girl, Jill! "

Andy shouted with laughter at the idea that Jill had been clever, and Jill was glad to laugh too, in a shaky sort of way.

They hurried down the hill and burst into the living room with their news. Of course Mr. Dallas wasn't home yet, but they could at least tell Mother. And maybe Adrian, if he felt like listening.

But the moment they entered the living room they knew that trouble was breaking. Adrian was being openly rude to Mother.

" Go ahead if you want to! " he was saying. " But just count me out. If Dad wants to take the rest of you to Fisherman's Wharf for dinner tonight — O.K. But I don't want to be in on any sort of make-believe family party. You've turned my father against me, and this isn't a family! We didn't want you here in the first place, and you needn't think — "

He didn't get any further because Andy crossed the room with a determination that sent Carol squealing out of the way. He grabbed his brother by the collar.

" You take that back! You take it back or I'm going to shove it right down your throat! "

Adrian shook his brother's hands aside angrily. But before he could say another word, or Andy could grab him again, Mother was between them. She looked very tiny and helpless as she pushed at each boy with her small hands. But Mother was angry too this time. Angrier than Jill had ever seen her and it was a startling sight.

" You can both stop it right now! " Mother cried.

Both boys were taken by surprise. They couldn't reach for each other without hurting Mother, and she kept right on pushing a hand against each boy's chest.

When she had them separated, she pointed sternly to chairs on opposite sides of the room. " Sit down," she ordered. " Both of you. You too, Jill. And stop crying, Carol. Nobody's hurting you."

Jill felt a little like crying herself and laughing at the same time. Mother looked like a tiny lion tamer, cracking an imaginary whip to make two growling beasts return to their posts.

" Now then," Mother said, " we're going to have a talk. We're going to stop being angry, stop throwing our emotions around blindly, and try to use our heads. And that means me too."

She took a long deep breath before she continued, as if she were trying to quiet her own impulse to anger.

" Adrian, Andy, don't you think I know how you feel about having the girls and me come into this house? You loved your mother a great deal and it has been only two years since you lost her. Of course you'd resent anyone who tried to take her place and pretend to be your mother. You might even feel that it would be disloyal to your mother to like me. Isn't that right? "

Andy shook his head unhappily. " I like you fine," he said. Adrian stared at his shoes and didn't speak.

Mother gave Andy a smile of thanks and went on. " But you don't need to feel disloyal to your mother, because I'm not trying to take her place. I couldn't be your mother if I wanted to. But what I hope to be is your good friend. I'm not trying to turn your dad against you, Adrian. Only you could do that. He isn't going to like it if you're unkind to me, any more than he'd like it if I were unkind to you. He loves you and wants to care for you both to the best of his ability. All I ask is a chance to add my own love and care to his. I don't think I deserve to be hated for that."

Adrian wriggled in his chair, his expression resistant and stormy.

Mother went on quickly. " Part of growing up means growing to think about other people, as well as about yourself. You four will all grow up and have your own lives and you'll begin to give yourselves to others. Later on you won't need parents as much as you do now. Then where will your father be? Where will I be? Pretty lonesome, don't you think? That's why we need each other too. So we won't be alone later when you've gone. That's all a family is — some people who need each other and want to love and help each other. Well — that's all I have to say, but I hope you'll think it over. I hope you'll even try to think of how your mother would have wanted it to be. I don't think she'd have wished unhappiness for any of us. From what I've heard of her, she was a pretty fine person. But I don't want to be Margaret, your mother. I only want to be Emily, your friend."

Then, all of a sudden, Mother stopped being brave and started to cry. She jumped up and ran upstairs to her bedroom without a backward look. Only Carol ran after her.

Adrian didn't say a word, or look at Jill or Andy. He disappeared behind his screen and they heard him fiddling with his painting things. Jill picked up a book and pretended to read, but she couldn't make any sense of the words because of the thoughts that kept whirling through her head. Andy stood at the window staring across the Bay.

After a while Mother came downstairs with Carol and, except for a little pinkness under the powder on her nose, she looked as if nothing had happened.

"You haven't told me a word about your visit to Miss Lydia," she said. Mother, Jill felt, was a most astonishing and wonderful person.

So they told her and even Andy got talkative and related what had happened after the tremor when Jill had run to get the cat. Carol squealed at his description of the moment when Jill had tripped over the doorsill. But it was Jill who told about the message from Karl von Wallenstein. Mother was entranced with the whole story. Of course Roger must write this for his paper, she said. San Franciscans would love it, and it would mean so much to Miss Lydia to have the truth told.

Before Mr. Dallas came home they had all changed their clothes and were ready for dinner at Fisherman's Wharf. All except Adrian. He simply grunted when Andy called to him and said gruffly, " I'm busy."

Mother shook her head at Adrian's father and put a finger to her lips. They all went out of the house, leaving him behind, and Jill felt almost sorry for him. But if he wasn't going to accept Mother's words and get over his bad temper, it served him right to be left behind without any coaxing.

In the car Mother said quietly that Adrian needed some time to think, and they all ought to let him alone and not say a word.

Fisherman's Wharf was a wonderful place. There were a number of wooden wharfs with water lapping their posts and sucking at the sides of boats anchored in the enclosure. There were so many boats that their spars and masts stuck up like a toothpick forest. Walks led along the piers and there was a line of open shops, selling everything from shells to postcards. Crabs were cooked in kettles right on the walks, and women were buying them for the evening meal.

There were smells too and Carol wrinkled up her nose, but to Jill this was the odor of adventure, and she loved it. Fish from all the seas, and the pungent briny smell of the sea itself, made up of so many different things. They sat at a big table right over the water and a row of sea gulls watched them from the roof of a nearby shed. In the background rose the tall hills of San Francisco.

While they ate savory sea food dishes, Jill and Andy

told their story of the afternoon's adventures again.
Mr. Dallas practically stopped eating to listen and he
had a better idea on this than anyone else.

" After all," he said, his eyes twinkling with lively
interest, " if your Miss Lydia used to be a writer, why
shouldn't she write this story herself? I could help her
a bit to get a modern slant, and perhaps do an introduction that would give some of the background of the
whole story. But I think her words might please our
readers most. And it might give her a lot of satisfac-
tion to write it."

He liked the idea of photographs too — of the house
and the two sisters, and of Hana, Jill, and Andy. It was
too bad the green cat was broken, or they could have
used a photograph of that. He would take the matter
up with his editor the very next day.

He was still talking when Jill happened to glance up
and see Adrian standing in the doorway of the little
restaurant, looking toward them hesitantly. This was
not the cocky, independent Adrian she had seen so
many times in the past few weeks. This boy was young
and worried and uncertain.

Roger Dallas saw his son at the same moment and
the smile left his face. This time, Jill knew, he was going to be very angry with Adrian for his recent behavior. She touched her mother's arm so that Emily turned
her head and saw Adrian. This was something only
Mother could deal with and she would need to do
something quickly.

It was Adrian, however, who moved first. He did not
look at his father or brother, or at the two girls, but

only at Emily. All his uncertainty and sorryness and apology were directed at her as plainly as though he had put them into words. Yet Adrian, who talked so easily, did not seem to know what to say. He crossed the room and stood anxiously beside Emily's chair.

" Is — is there room for me? " he asked.

There was no time for Mr. Dallas to be angry, for Emily spoke swiftly and sweetly.

" There's always room for you, Adrian," she said and her smile was the warm smile of a loving friend.

Across the table Roger Dallas relaxed and Jill sensed that he knew a sincere apology had been made by his son, even though it had not been put into words, and that his wife had accepted it fully.

The waiter brought a chair and Adrian slipped into place beside Carol, rumpling her hair with an affectionate hand, just as any brother might do. He carried a portfolio, which he leaned against his chair until after his order had been given. Then he picked it up and opened it.

" I — I had a job to finish," he said, still hesitant, and held up the picture for them to see.

Jill gasped. There, painted in pale, soft green, was Miss Lydia's cat. The proud, raised head, the lips pulled back from snarling fangs, the elongated body and the tail curled around puffy forepaws, were all exactly right. But there was more than that. Adrian had caught in his picture the same mysterious suggestion of life that the china figure had carried — as if at any moment the creature might move on the paper and stretch itself like any cat.

" This is really wonderful! " Mother said in rapt approval.

Adrian did not shrug her praise aside. " Thank you, Emily," he said, sounding surprisingly respectful and grateful. " Since the real cat got broken, I thought Miss Lydia might like to have a picture of it to keep."

Jill carried the suggestion one step farther. " Mr. Dallas, maybe a picture of Adrian's cat could be printed along with the newspaper story? "

" It certainly could," he agreed. He reached out and gave her a quick approving pat on the arm, and she knew how relieved and pleased he was about Adrian.

Adrian smiled a little sheepishly at Jill. " Thanks for the publicity. But, look — if I can call your mother ' Emily,' don't you think it's about time you started calling my father ' Roger '? "

Jill blushed and glanced shyly at Mr. Dallas.

Adrian's father was smiling at her. " Hi, Jill," he said.

She gathered up all her courage. " Hi, Roger," said Jill. And she was over the hump. She had said it out loud and it would never again be as hard as the first time.

The waiter brought Adrian's order and everyone began to eat again. Jill, stealing a quick look around the busy table, felt happier than she had at any time since she and Carol had come to San Francisco. She had a feeling that Adrian had finally got himself turned around so that he was heading in the right direction. And that he liked it.

For the first time the group didn't seem to be separated into two halves of different families, but were just one family together. They were truly friends now, and for each other.

How good this crab tasted, Jill thought, and knew it was because happiness gave everything added flavor.